BROWN COW

BROWN COW

by

John Branfield

LONDON
VICTOR GOLLANCZ LTD
1983

British Library Cataloguing in Publication Data
Branfield, John
    Brown cow.
    I. Title
    823'.914[J]   PZ7
    ISBN 0-575-03223-5

Printed in Great Britain at
The Camelot Press Ltd, Southampton

For Steve and Debbie

Part One

They walked through the shade beneath the trees towards the band of sunlight, where hundreds of girls frolicked in knickers and blouses. They could hear the high, excited chatter and laughter, the cries of encouragement.

"I want to go back," said Andy. He felt weak at the knees as they waded through the long grass. "I don't think we ought to be here."

"I'm not missing this," said Reg.

"We ought to have come the other way."

"It's all right. Don't worry!"

Reg was slightly ahead. No one had seen them yet; in their school uniform of black blazers and grey flannels they were well camouflaged amongst the holly and laurel bushes, and the girls on the sports field had their backs to them, giving their attention to a race in progress on the track. Some of them were bobbing up and down and flapping their arms.

Andy caught a glimpse of running figures beyond the spectators, of fair hair flying and coloured ribbons. The shouting rose to a crescendo, and then there was a burst of applause.

They came out from beneath the trees and stood blinking in the sunshine. Andy pulled off his school cap and stuffed it into his blazer pocket; he felt embarrassed wearing a cap.

The race was over, and some of the girls began to move away. A few wore the brown and white check dresses which were the summer uniform of the girls' grammar school, but most were wearing cream-coloured aertex blouses and dark-brown gym knickers. They swarmed everywhere, in all shapes and sizes. There were too many; he couldn't take them all in at once. He tried to pick out one to focus on. A ginger-haired girl was talking very animatedly about the result of the race, and as she talked she eased the elastic around the top of her legs. But then others got in the way, dancing across his field of vision, and he followed them.

He had seen girls before, at the public baths on Sunday mornings; there they were in swimming costumes and he didn't take quite so much notice of them (although he still noticed them, of course). But these girls looked as though they were in their underclothes. He couldn't keep his eyes still.

In his experience the whole object of parents and teachers was to keep girls covered up. He wouldn't have been surprised if they had been made to dress like nuns or muslim women with yashmaks over their faces. And now here they were, hundreds of them, uncovered before him.

"Strewth!" breathed Reg.

They stood at the edge of the sports field and gawped.

Suddenly Andy realised that two girls had detached themselves from the crowd and were waving to them. They had been seen. He felt a moment of panic, of wanting to run away again.

The girls were coming towards them. The one in front was very tall, even lanky; her fair, plaited hair was done up in a coil on top of her head. Her legs were very white, and she was so skinny that her pants hung loose on her. The other girl was about average height, with shoulder-length dark hair. She filled her clothes, rounding them out plumply.

As the girls approached them, his eyes zoomed from one to the other, bouncing off legs, knickers and blouses. He

8

made an effort to keep them fixed on the girl in front.

"You're the boys from the grammar school," she called.

"That's right," said Reg.

"I'm Dorothy Best," she said, holding out her hand. "And this is Gloria Butterfield."

"We've been sent to meet you," said Gloria.

The girls pretended that there was nothing unusual about the situation, but they were as conscious of being without their ordinary clothes as the boys were. They tried to make it seem the most normal thing in the world, and then they laughed awkwardly and didn't know what to do with their hands.

"Thanks for the invitation," said Reg. He looked the girls up and down cheekily. "I definitely approve."

"It was Miss Baraclough's idea. She thinks there should be more contact between the schools."

"I approve of that too."

"So do we!"

They laughed again, and then they all started moving away from the trees towards the race track. Andy glanced around him, and his eyes did a quick double-take. For there on the grass, a few feet away, was a girl who had taken part in the race and who had now flopped down exhausted. She was sitting with her head back, her arms propped stiffly behind her. Her blouse clung to her, and she wasn't wearing a bra. He could see where her nipples were.

He couldn't have stopped looking, even if he were to be led away to immediate execution for not averting his gaze. The others followed his eyes. "Are you all right, Julie?" the girls called.

Her chest was rising and falling as she panted for breath. She smiled between gritted teeth, and nodded gamely.

"What was the race?" he asked, making himself speak. "What distance?"

"A quarter of a mile."

"I thought it must have been at least a mile."

"They don't allow us to run a mile, it's not good for girls." Dorothy spoke sarcastically, as though she wouldn't mind having a go.

"I bet you're good at the high jump," said Reg, looking at her long legs.

"Long jump actually," she said.

"Dorothy's beaten the school record," said Gloria. "She'll probably be *victrix ludorum*."

"What's that?" asked Reg, with put-on dumbness.

"The sports day champion," said Andy. Then he explained to the girls. "He hasn't done any Latin. Our School's only just started it again. They dropped it for the duration."

"Lucky you!" the girls laughed.

"Most of the teachers went away for the war."

"I wish ours had!"

"They're coming back now though. And twice as keen as ever."

Dorothy had to take them to the headmistress, and they walked towards the starting line. There were girls everywhere, standing around waiting for the next race or sitting on the grass, making daisy chains or eating ice-cream. They looked curiously at the boys as they passed, and giggled. One girl was stretched out on her tummy, her bottom in the air.

"Wow!" thought Andy as he stepped carefully over her legs. And to think that they had been invited to come, that it was all official. Suddenly the world was topsy-turvy.

There were a few adults amongst the spectators, mostly mothers and one or two fathers, local shopkeepers from Barnsby, taking the afternoon off to watch their daughters – and their daughters' friends. Andy could tell that they were interested by the way they pretended not to be. Like the two girls, they were being more ordinary than normal, more bluff and hearty and generally making it quite clear that they were there because they supported the school and their daughters' education. They weren't mucky-minded young lads; they were solid Yorkshire businessmen. They weren't looking at anybody's legs.

On the way the boys were introduced to more of the senior girls; there was Margery who was freckled and Beverley who was all teeth and June who was "bustin' out all over". Valerie was all right. Nora, Betty, Doris – he couldn't remember everyone's name.

Eventually they came to the line, where the headmistress held the starting pistol. It flashed through Andy's mind that she was going to shoot him, that this was why he had been brought here. (He felt he deserved to be shot.)

"Which of you is Willoughby?" she asked, passing the pistol into her other hand.

Reg smoothed back his hair with a spiv-like gesture and said how-do-you-do.

She turned to Andy. "And you must be *Trew*in."

"Tre*win*," said Andy automatically, changing the accent from the first syllable of his name to the second.

"I'm glad you've come," she said. "I'd like to see the boys' and girls' schools getting together more often."

"Yes," said Reg.

"We've gone our separate ways in the past, but in the new world we shall have to co-operate much more. We shall have to get to know each other and share each other's interests."

Brave new world, thought Andy.

"I hope the girls are looking after you," she added, looking at Dorothy and Gloria.

"Yes, Miss Baraclough," they chorused.

"Splendid." She dismissed them with a wave.

They wandered over to the high jump. It was very amateurish, without even a sandpit, and instead of a crossbar there was a length of rope held down at each end by a pear-shaped weight (or breast-shaped, as Andy thought). The rope sagged in the middle, giving an extra three inches to the competitor.

By now he was getting used to being surrounded by girls, and he began to take more notice of Gloria. She was smashing. He thought of all the questions he could ask her. Where did she live? What subjects was she doing? Did she like going to the pictures?

"Are you prefects?" she asked, before he had said anything.

"No, we're in the lower sixth," he said eagerly. In the lower sixth they were only monitors. "The prefects are all in the upper sixth, they couldn't come because they're preparing for their exams."

"Oh." She sounded disappointed.

"The Old Man thought it would be too distracting for them," said Reg. "The sight of all these thighs might drive them frantic."

"He sent us instead," said Andy.

"He knew he could trust us."

" 'Look here, lads,' he said. 'Girls' school have invited sixth form to sports day. I'm sending you to keep up reputation of Bywaters. Don't forget, lads, you're ambassadors for t' school.' "

Andy enjoyed doing imitations of Old Man Harding. He liked trying out his Yorkshire accent, and he didn't want Reg always to have the last word. Reg was very successful with girls (at least, by his own account). He wanted Gloria to notice *him*.

A competitor came thundering up to the posts, stopped, did a standing jump, and ended up with the rope tangled round her legs. It was embarrassing. They moved on and watched some first-year events. Andy didn't find first-formers very interesting.

"Come on, Nightingale!" cried a middle-aged teacher.

"Is that a person or a house?" he asked Gloria. He was standing close to her.

"I thought it was a bird," said Reg, acting dumb again.

"It's a house," she said.

"Are the other houses birds?"

"No, stupid," said Gloria. "They're famous women."

12

"Nightingale, Fry, Darling and Curie," said Dorothy scornfully. "Terribly unimaginative really."

"At the boys' school they're Carson, Thwaite, Rowley and Snell," said Gloria. A different tone came into her voice when she spoke about the boys' school.

"It sounds like a firm of solicitors." Andy was as scornful as Dorothy had been.

"They're named after benefactors of the school," said Gloria.

"How do you know that?"

"Oh, I know a lot about Bywaters," she said mysteriously.

They watched Dorothy win the long jump, and when it was over they even had a jump themselves, which made them popular with the spectators. (Neither of them reached her mark.) She went on to win the half-mile, in which Gloria took part but dropped out, red-faced, after two laps.

Then they had tea. The senior girls had set a table in the shade of a tree, and on it were cucumber sandwiches and slices of fruit cake; they brought kettles and a teapot from the school. Andy and Reg sat on a grassy slope, balancing plates and cups, surrounded by girls. They felt like sultans in the East.

Gloria stared across the playing fields. "I wish I went to the boys' school," she said.

"Eh?" said both boys incredulously.

She plucked a piece of grass, sliding it out of its stem and then biting the end with her pouting lips. "It's so stupid at this place." She knitted her dark eyebrows together, and a frown creased her forehead. Her hair fell over her face, and she tossed it back.

"It's all so petty," said Dorothy. "'Yes, Miss Baraclough. No, Miss Baraclough'. They aren't interested in our education, they just want us to be well-behaved little girls."

"It's pretty stupid at the boys' school," said Andy. "It's

13

the same really, they just want you to be one sort of person."

"But at least it's something. You *want* to win your races at sports day, you *want* to win scholarships to Oxford and Cambridge. We just play at it. It's pathetic." Her cheeks were pink and her eyes came to life beneath her pale lashes.

"It must be wonderful to be a prefect at the boys' school," said Gloria.

The boys laughed out loud.

"And to be head boy must be most wonderful of all."

They couldn't believe their ears. "Do you know him?" asked Andy.

"Jeremy Duckworth," she said, repeating his name like a charm. "He's captain of rugby . . . and captain of cricket . . . and *victor ludorum* at sports day."

Reg and Andy both groaned. Jeremy Duckworth was no friend of theirs.

"I think he's super," said Gloria. She rolled over, turning away from them. There were bits of dried grass sticking to her knickers, and the backs of her legs were criss-crossed with tiny indentations from the blades on which she had been sitting.

When she same out of school, Gloria had changed into her brown and white gingham dress and a brown blazer. Some of the girls coming down the driveway wore straw boaters, but her hair was free. She seemed so much older that it startled him. He would never have dared ask to ride home with her if she had looked like this. He wondered how he had found the courage as it was.

He sat waiting on his bike, alongside the low wall where the railings had been before they were taken for the war effort. She wheeled her bicycle up to him.

"How now?" he said as she approached.

"Brown cow," she said wearily, as though she had heard it a thousand times before. It was the traditional taunt from the Bywaters boys, because of the grammar school uniform.

They cycled along the Huddersfield Road. Their homes were in the same direction, though he had never seen her before. The boys had to leave much earlier in the morning to catch the train, and got back long after the girls had left school.

"You're not Yorkshire," she said. She had more of an accent when she spoke outside the school. "Where do you come from?"

He remembered the catechisms he'd had when he first arrived at the boys' school. "What do they call you?" they kept saying. He thought it was some sort of joke.

"Cornwall," he answered.

"What are you doing in Yorkshire?"

"My dad came here to work." He worked in a government office and towards the end of the war he had to move.

"Do you like it?" she asked. (He knew what would come next.)

"It's all right," he said. An RAF transporter roared by, carrying the fuselage of a plane, a Gloster Meteor.

"What did you say?" she shouted.

"I said it's all right. It's not as good as Cornwall."

She was affronted. "Yorkshire's best," she said with absolute certainty.

"How do you know?" he said. "You can only say it's best if you've been to Cornwall.

"I don't need to," she said.

He dropped behind her as another load of aeroplane parts went by. He looked at her legs turning the pedals. They were very brown above her white socks. She leaned slightly from side to side as she rode.

"Yorkshire's best for cricket," she said as he drew level with her again. "Cornwall haven't even got a team."

"They have."

"They aren't in the county championship."

"I'm not talking about cricket," said Andy.

15

But Gloria was, and she wouldn't let go of the subject. "Which is the county nearest to Cornwall in the championship?"

"Somerset, I suppose."

"Somerset!" she exclaimed, "Yorkshire beat Somerset at Headingly. If they played Cornwall they would *slay* them."

They had passed the rows of terraces, and the big detached houses set back from the road in large gardens behind lilac bushes and laburnam trees. They rattled over the level crossing, and were now passing the semi-detached houses which had been built just before the war.

"That's where I live," he said, nodding at a house where all the woodwork was camouflage green.

"Just think, I pass it every day," she said.

"I'll look out for you."

His dad was home, his bike was leaning against the wall. They rode straight by. There were gaps between the houses now, and the sites where the building had stopped were used as allotments.

"Somerset!" said Gloria scathingly.

They continued to wrangle about Yorkshire and the south-west until they came to open country. There were cornfields on either side, with red poppies growing amongst the rye, and ahead of them one large oak tree at the end of a lane. On either side of the lane was a row of semi-detached houses. They looked incongruous, a bit of the town dropped down in the country. No doubt if it had not been for the war, they would have linked up with the rest. This was where Gloria lived.

She freewheeled to her gate, and got off, catching her skirt on the seat. She stood and smoothed down her dress. Andy slewed his bike around, and sat with one foot on the ground.

"What are you doing tonight?" he asked.

"Homework," she said emphatically.

"On sports day?"

"They didn't let us off."

"Well, I'll see you around." He looked at her bike. "You want to lower your saddle a bit," he said, dropping his hand on to it. Then he took if off, because it suddenly seemed a very intimate gesture.

He sped home. He pushed his bike through the weeds of the side garden, and put it away in the shed. He unfastened his satchel from the crossbar – he didn't like wearing it over his shoulder, any more than he liked wearing a cap – and swung it just above the ground as he entered the house.

His mum and dad were having tea and listening to the six o'clock news on the wireless. "How did you get on?" they asked, turning down the volume.

"All right," he said. They were quite proud that he had been chosen to represent the school. Privately, he thought that Harding had chosen Reg and himself to show that he didn't take the invitation seriously. More contact between the schools was the last thing he wanted, and sending *them* was an insult to Miss Baraclough.

He sat down at the table. Although they had lived here three years, the furniture still seemed out of place. It belonged in Cornwall. It had come up by rail, and had taken nearly a month to be delivered. It had hung around in sidings during the day, moving by night to avoid the bombers. It had been held back to let the troop trains, the coal and the ammunition through, and had been diverted around devastated cities and damaged track. It always impressed Andy that their few ordinary bits and pieces had made this heroic journey.

Once they had arrived, his parents had done nothing to make them look as though they belonged. The previous owner worked at the air force base; he must have had access to unlimited supplies of ministry paint, because the whole house, inside and out, was painted in camouflage colours of khaki and dark green, and a bright yellow which had probably been used in the airmen's barracks. His mum and dad hadn't altered anything.

They hadn't wanted to come to Yorkshire, and within a week his dad had put in for a transfer back to Cornwall. It was only a matter of time now; meanwhile everything seemed temporary, as though they were just camping out and waiting.

His parents were like displaced persons, like refugees from eastern Europe. They didn't even speak the language, and although the neighbours were friendly they took it as an insult that they went back to Cornwall at every opportunity. Andy had never spent any of the holidays in Yorkshire; as soon as the term finished, he and his mother went to stay with his mother's sister near Truro. They only came back for the new term. Mr Trewin joined them for as long as he had leave, and looked after himself in Barnsby for the rest of the time.

After tea Andy went up to his bedroom, one of the rooms painted with dark green gloss paint. He set up the green baize-topped card-table on which he did his homework, and wrote an essay on the comic style of Chaucer. He was distracted by pictures of Brown Cows which kept appearing before his mind, a girl jiggling up and down in excitement as she watched a race, a girl landing feet foremost in the long jump and toppling on to her back, a girl breasting the tape at the end of the hundred yards. However, he finished the essay. He thought he had made quite a good job of it in the circumstances. Alpha minus, if he was lucky.

When he was in bed his mind kept returning to Gloria. He thought about everything that she had said. He wondered what she had meant about Duckworth. She couldn't be serious, she had never spoken to him. He'd have to find out more.

He'd never been out with a girl. He wasn't like Reg, he didn't want just anybody. He'd like to go out with Gloria. He hoped he would see her again.

The station clock at Barnsby showed five past eight. The

York train had just steamed out, leaving piles of newspapers done up with string on the platform. The bookstall opened and Andy collected the *Daily Express* for the school library. He crossed the footbridge to the other side, where the train for Bywaters was waiting, and found an empty compartment. He slung his satchel up on to the rack, and sat by the door. He rested a foot on the opposite seat so that his leg would stop any unwanted person from entering, and opened the paper.

He glanced up, and dropped his leg to let Reg Willoughby come in. Reg took a comb out of his breast pocket and passed it through his wavy Brylcreemed hair, peering into the cracked mirror on one side of the compartment.

Andy swopped his *Daily Express* for Reg's *Daily Mirror*, and turned to *Jane*, the strip cartoon in which the heroine nearly always fell into some predicament which left her undressed. She was in her bath today, making a telephone call.

"Heck, I don't want this one," said Reg, and he took back his *Mirror*.

Reg swore that the man who drew *Jane* was his uncle. He had two models to pose for him, he said; one for the top half and one for the legs. He claimed that he had been in his uncle's studio when the bottom half was posing.

"It's very odd," he said, putting on the man-of-the-world touch. "You see her there stark naked, and you don't turn a hair. Then you come outside and you see a girl bending over to pump up her bicycle tyre and you give a whistle."

You could never really believe what Reg said. He claimed that the photographer in Lennard Road was another uncle of his. During the war women used to ask him to take pin-up photos of themselves to send to their husbands or boy-friends. Reg had gone through his files one day; he said half the women of Barnsby were there, all in the nude. He'd seen them all.

Some younger boys came along, and tried to enter the carriage. They always tried to get in with a member of the public if they could, though usually the only passengers on the train were boys going to school. Often a passenger would settle himself comfortably in an empty compartment, and then to his surprise about twenty youngsters – of whom there'd been no sign a moment before – would try to crush in with him, standing packed between the seats.

If there were no adults on the train, they tried to travel with the sixth-formers, with whom they knew they were safe. But Reg held the door-handle firm.

"Go on, Willoughby," they pleaded. "Let us in."

"Up the train," he said, jerking his thumb.

"Jackson says he's going to get us."

"Get moving."

"Be a sport."

He shook his head. If you let them in, you were swamped with them; you couldn't even read your paper, or finish off your homework from last night.

The engine gave a roar and let out a cloud of smoke. The first-formers were startled, and moving as one like a swarm of fish, darted into compartments further down the train. Steam rose between the platform and the wheels; the guard blew his whistle.

There was a great banging of doors. Jackson and his mob came out of their compartment and followed the first-formers, who raised cries of alarm. One or two escaped, rushed frantically up and down the platform, and were pulled through open doors. Everyone was at the windows. Some third-year boys thought it would be a good idea to take over the compartment that Jackson had vacated. They changed over; the guard shouted, a porter slammed doors, and the wheels began to turn.

"They're not going to make it," said Reg, leaning out of the window.

Then there was a great hollow drumming noise, as several people tore across the covered footway, the tread of their feet echoing in the enclosed space. They leapt down the stairs, half a dozen steps at a time, and raced along the platform.

The train began to pick up speed. Reg opened the door and called. As they drew level they shot their satchels into the compartment as though they were making rugger passes, and dived in themselves. Reg grabbed them by the coat or trousers, and hauled them aboard: Braithwaite, Thornton, Pickles and Rayner. Pugsley wasn't a prefect, but he always went around with them.

The last one of all was Duckworth, a big overgrown lad who was only just keeping level with the train. His arms and legs were going like pistons. The end of the platform was coming up. He got one large hand around the side of the door, a foot on to the step, and swung himself in. Reg shut the door as the platform swept out of sight.

Duckworth immediately turned and leaned his gaunt face out of the window.

"Get your heads in!" he bellowed. "Burton, come to the study at break." All heads disappeared at once inside the windows.

The prefects were on board. Everyone else was expected to arrive early; if you were a prefect you were expected to arrive at the last possible moment. No one had ever written this down, or even said so; it was part of the ritual of Bywaters School.

The train jolted over the points, and then began the climb up on to the embankment, which ran as straight as an arrow through the open fields to the wayside halt near the school, some seven miles away.

A shriek came from further down the train, and a voice shouted clearly, "No, Jackson. Please don't do it. Please, Jackson, please."

Duckworth and Pugsley laughed.

It was all a joke. Nobody was really being hurt, the kids were only play-acting. They wouldn't thank you if you kept them separate, because they wanted to get in with Jackson. They enjoyed it.

It had always been like this. In fact in the past it had been much worse. When Duckworth had been in the first form they had really suffered. People working in the fields would look up and see the train, high on the embankment, with a small boy held by the legs hanging out of a window. He had once seen a first-former bundled up and transferred through the windows from one compartment to the next. In his first year, a kid had been tied to the luggage rack and left there all day, travelling to and fro along the branch line, until he was taken down in the evening on their way home. Passengers were always being startled by the face of a boy at the window as he walked along the outside of the train, either by choice or under pressure. To listen to Duckworth, it must have once looked like trains in India, with as many passengers on the outside as within.

It had become very tame since the war.

A series of blood-curdling screams could be heard above the beat of the wheels. The cries went on and on and Andy felt sorry for the kids who were being bullied. He knew it wasn't a joke, you only had to see their faces as they darted about the platform to know that they were terrified. One or two of them, perhaps, found it exciting. But most of them were dead scared.

There had always been rough-houses on the train, and nobody wanted to stop them. The prefects had grown up with the system and now they were at the top, it suited them for it to remain the same. The parents didn't want to change it; they were proud of Bywaters School, it was part of the community and its traditions. Andy was glad that he had never been a junior at the school.

The train pulled in to the halt. There was no sign of any village, just miles and miles of flat fields with a few clumps of trees, under an enormous sky. If you looked carefully you could see a church spire rising out of one of the clumps, and behind the trees was the village and Bywaters School. Andy had wondered where he was coming to, the first time he arrived.

Doors were opening, and boys jumping out before the

train came to a stop. There was a rush for the gate and the slope down the embankment; everyone wanted to get to the front. The sixth-formers waited on the platform until all the others had left.

"Get your tie on," snapped Duckworth to a small boy who staggered out of Jackson's compartment, his clothes dishevelled.

"Jackson, give me my tie back," he said, emboldened by Duckworth's presence.

Jackson glanced at the head boy, and returned the tie. The kid ran off, trying to get his tie on and catch up the others at the same time. The sixth form followed down the slope. The engine puffed along the embankment, hauling its two carriages towards the distant horizon. The sky was a clear blue.

"It's time we had a mush," Duckworth announced.

Once they were under the bridge and in the lane, the prefects tore switches out of the hedgerow. Some of the boys saw what was happening and began to run, and their running started off others.

The prefects started up a cry of "Moosh, moosh!" and charged at the backs of the runners, brandishing their switches.

Andy and Reg stood aside to let them pass.

"Come on, you two!" shouted Duckworth.

"I'm not running," said Andy.

"Bloody stupid," said Reg.

Duckworth swirled his piece of branch, still with the leaves on it, but didn't bring it near them. "I'll see you later," he said, and tore on to catch up with the others.

They herded the train-boys along the lane, driving them with their sticks as though they were teams of dogs, and the cry of "Moosh, moosh!" was taken up by all the runners as they swept on towards the village.

It was quiet behind the mush, though they could hear it roaring ahead, and it was pleasant not to be tramping along in a cloud of dust with about a hundred others around you. The hedges were full of dog-roses, and they each picked one and put them in their buttonholes.

Andy had a free period before break, so he left the library early and went to the prefect's study, which was a pokey hole of a place, but it had a few battered armchairs and some shelves to put your books on, and it wasn't a bad refuge unless it was crowded with prefects and monitors. Andy had the right to use it because he was a monitor, a sort of sub-prefect. He hadn't told Gloria, because he found it about as embarrassing as wearing a cap and carrying a satchel slung from his shoulder.

There was one other boy there, a Lithuanian refugee called Pavel. He had arrived as a boarder at the beginning of the year, speaking no English; he was learning fast, and was supposed to be a brilliant scientist. Andy felt they had a lot in common; they were both outsiders and he would have liked to know him better, but he was difficult to talk to.

The best thing about the study, apart from the coal fire in winter, was the gas ring on which you could make coffee, and there was plenty of free school milk. He made a mug for himself and one for Pavel. They set up a game of chess across the corner of the table.

The place quickly filled up when the bell rang, and people were soon sitting on the arms of the chairs and high up on the window ledges. Andy and Pavel were hemmed in around their chess board; Andy began the opening for a fool's-mate, knowing Pavel wouldn't be taken in by it. Duckworth came in and his pile of books was passed wobbling from person to person until the last person dumped them on the shelf, and threw him his tin of coffee. Everyone was talking loudly.

"There's a kid to see you," shouted the latest person to come through the door.

"Tell him to wait," shouted Duckworth.

He made his coffee, and stood drinking it in front of the

empty grate. "Let's have him," he said, and Pugsley brought the boy in.

He was an untidy, scruffy-looking kid from the third form. He glanced like a trapped animal at all the older boys ranged around him, and then turned his head sideways and looked into the fireplace. Everyone stopped talking.

"You know why you're here, Burton," said Duckworth.

"Yes."

"You tell me why."

"I was looking out of the window."

"You weren't looking out of the window," Duckworth said. "You had your head out of the window. And that's a very dangerous thing to do, isn't it?"

"Yes."

"You know what the penalty is," said Duckworth. He stretched across three or four heads to reach his shelf, and picked up his size ten gym slipper. "Bend over."

The boy didn't move.

"Come on, I haven't got all day."

"I can't," he said between clenched teeth.

"Why not?"

He said something so quietly that Duckworth couldn't hear him.

"Speak up!"

"I've got boils," he whispered.

Pugsley laughed.

"Do you expect me to believe that?" asked Duckworth.

"It's true."

"Show me your medical certificate."

"Medical certificate?"

"Yes, your medical certificate to prove it."

"I haven't got one."

Andy felt uncomfortable. "Come off it, Duckworth," he said. "How could he get a medical certificate? He didn't know he was going to get into trouble."

"Then he should have taken extra care, shouldn't he?"

"He only had his head out of the window like a lot of other people."

"Shut up, *Trew*in. I'll deal with this." He turned back to the boy. "I don't believe you're telling the truth, Burton, and there's only one way to find out. Take down your trousers."

"It's true, honest it is."

"Prove it."

The boy hesitated, then bent over and touched his toes. "All right, Duckworth. Go on, hit me."

Duckworth looked round. "He was only trying it on," he said. "You would have believed him, *Trew*in."

He swept his arm round to clear a space. "Come on, give me some room. You couldn't swing a cat in here."

He swung the slipper with all his force. The boy leaped forward and yelled, clutching his trousers. "Now you've done it," he screamed. "You've bloody broken it, it's all bleeding."

"Come on, bend over again," said Duckworth.

Burton was almost hysterical. "You'll have to explain it to the doctor," he shouted. "He'll want to see you. You've done it now."

Duckworth swung again, but pulled back at the last moment. He gave him one more tap, and told him to go. Burton turned round at the door, his face tear-stained and angry. "You'll hear more about this, Duckworth. I wouldn't like to be in your shoes." He slammed the door.

"He was putting it on," said Duckworth. "It was just an act."

Andy had watched Pavel throughout the incident. He sat studying the chess board, countering Andy's opening attack and slowly drinking his coffee. His face showed nothing at all. What did he make of it? He had been through the camps of eastern Europe. What did he really think of English schools? Andy wondered.

"I'd like a word with you, *Trew*in," said Duckworth when

the bell went for the end of break. He cornered him and Reg as they were about to leave.

"Tre*win*," said Andy.

"You two are getting very bolshy these days. Why didn't you take part in the mush this morning? Why did you speak up for that kid just now?"

"I thought he was telling the truth."

"He was lying, I proved it."

"He might have been exaggerating, but I think he probably –"

"My God, *Trew*in," exclaimed Duckworth. "They'd twist you around their little fingers. It doesn't matter whether he was lying or not, I expect you to back me up in future."

"I've got an English lesson," said Andy, trying to push by.

Duckworth barred the way. "What are you wearing those flowers for?" he asked.

"We felt like it."

"You look like a couple of pansies."

"What about Founder's Day?" Everyone wore flowers on Founder's Day.

"That's Founder's Day, this isn't," said Duckworth. "It's not part of school uniform."

"I don't see the difference."

"Look here, *Trew*in," said Duckworth, using a favourite phrase of the Old Man's. "You like to be different, don't you? You don't fit in. If we all took your attitude the whole place would fall to pieces. You're slack, *Trew*in. It's time you set a better example."

"Pompous oaf!" said Reg. They had taken their sandwiches on to the cricket field, and were sitting eating them on the roller in the sun.

"You're slack, *Trew*in." Andy imitated Duckworth's accent.

"Quack, quack," went Reg.

They found Duckworth laughable because he was such a perfect product of the school. Bywaters was a grammar school, but being an ancient foundation and having boarding houses, it tried to be like a public school. It believed in all the public school qualities, perhaps even more so than a real public school. Things were done as they had always been done, and no one questioned authority.

Every Friday all boys from the fourth year upwards wore their air cadet uniforms and spent the afternoon doing basic training. The headmaster was the commanding officer, and there was no question of not doing it; no one had ever asked, it was inconceivable.

Andy would have liked to hand in the thick and itchy serge uniform, and resign his lance-corporal's stripe, gained for instructing others in the morse code. But if you went to Bywaters, you joined the ATC. Even Pavel was put into uniform.

It was all so rigid; there was no flexibility, no variety. And Duckworth was the most rigid of all. Other people kept back a little bit of themselves, but not Duckworth. In a few months' time he would join the Air Force to do his military service; he would come back and start work in his father's business. He would become a member of the Old Boys' Association, and play rugby for the Old Bywaterians. He would send his sons to the school, and they would grow up to be just like him. Duckworth practically *was* Bywaters School.

And this was the Duckworth that Gloria Butterfield dreamed of. She must be mad.

Major Tiny Lofthouse didn't hear the bell go, and he went on about Frederick the Great for five more minutes before anyone reminded him. Then they had to run for the train, and this time there was no question of Andy and Reg not feeling like it. If they missed this one they would have to wait three hours.

28

They ran down the centre of the road through the village, knowing they were the last, and turned into the lane to the station. They listened as they ran. If they didn't hear anything before they reached the clump of elms, they knew they would make it.

Just as they approached the trees, the cry went up from the boys already on the platform. They had seen smoke on the horizon. "Nix!" they called, cupping their hands like megaphones and dragging out the vowel for as long as they had breath. The traditional warning cry was taken up and called back by those still on the road. "Nix . . . nix . . . nix!"

The smaller boys broke into a gallop. The older boys calculated the time the train would take to reach the station, and the distance they still had to go, and set their pace accordingly. It was considered smart to judge it right.

Andy and Reg heard the cry, and increased their speed. They hugged their satchels under their arms, and raced flat out. They could hear the train now, and as they came into the last stretch it rattled over the bridge.

There was no one left on the road. They pounded down it, jackets flying. Under the bridge and up the slope. The engine hooted. The guard blew his whistle. The train moved. They dived into the nearest compartment.

When they got back to Barnsby station, the two girls were waiting in the road outside. They were sitting on their bicycles, looking as though they just happened to be passing.

"How now," said the boys.

"Oh, hullo," they said, pretending to be surprised to see them.

Dorothy looked different. Her hair was held back by a band and hung loosely on her shoulders, instead of being done up in plaits. She looked more attractive in a school dress and blazer, and with her hair free.

But Gloria looked super. Reg presented her with his now rather jaded dog-rose. Andy wished he had thought of it. She was delighted.

"Just think," she said, sniffing it rapturously. "It was growing in Bywaters this morning." She always went on as though Bywaters was some sort of Shangri-la. "Mmm . . . it's lovely!" Her Yorkshire accent was stronger than ever.

"It's a bit tired," said Reg.

"When I get home I'll put it in some water, with an aspirin. That'll revive it. I'll put it in my bedroom."

Andy felt that he ought to offer his limp dog-rose to Dorothy, which he did rather diffidently, and she accepted it. It was good to be standing there with them, after a day at school amongst crowds of boys.

Although she was so engrossed in the rose, Gloria was keeping her eyes on the station entrance. All the Bywaters boys had left, and dispersed into the town. She looked around. "Is there another way out?" she asked.

"No."

"Did anyone miss the train?"

"We nearly did," said Reg, and he told the story of how they had to run for it, but she wasn't listening.

"Where's Jeremy Duckworth?" she asked eventually.

"He had an exam this afternoon," said Andy, taking pleasure in his information. "It doesn't finish until five o'clock, he won't be back until seven."

"Oh." She looked disappointed.

"He was in a right state about it," said Reg. "Duckworth has got no –" He sought for the right word.

"Sang froid," said Andy.

"That's it," said Reg. "He was very touchy this morning."

"I bet he'll do better than you."

"What, our Gerry?" said Reg. "He's not one of the bright lads. He won't do as well as our Andy – he's a genius."

"Thanks, Reg."

"He's best at games," said Gloria. "He's captain of rugby and captain of cricket and *victor ludorum*." She could be really boring.

"Oh that!" they both scoffed.

"Well, I think he's super," she said.

They walked down the road to the public gardens, wheeling their bikes along the paths. All the lawns had been resown, after being dug up for the Dig for Victory campaign, and there were brightly-coloured flowerbeds. They propped their bikes against a shelter and sat down inside.

Gloria always wanted to talk about the boys' school. Her dad had been at the school and her brother was in the third form. She had a collection of sports day and Founder's Day programmes, and had knitted a scarf in the school colours. She was obsessed by the place.

They talked about teachers. All the pre-war masters had come back from the forces, and the women who had taken their places were going. There was only Maggie Thompson left, and she would be leaving at the end of the term.

"Do you remember when we used to read around the class?" said Reg. "Whenever we came to the word 'naked' we used to pronounce it '*naked*'." He said it as one syllable, to rhyme with *raked*, putting a lot of emphasis upon the word and speaking it with a strong Yorkshire accent. "Maggie didn't say a word, she just used to blush."

"When you cleaned the blackboard, you always put the board-rubber on the ledge at the top, so that she had to reach to get it. Her skirt would ride right up."

"You're awful," said Gloria, and both the girls laughed.

"It won't be the same when it's all men," said Andy sadly.

He didn't look forward to it. He liked Miss Thompson. Everyone pretended that she was unattractive, but he thought she was nice. Her face looked as though it had been moulded out of clay, and the sculptor had done it quickly with his thumb and had never properly finished it off. It sounded as though it should be ugly, and yet it was attractive. She had a nose like a spoon, and her breasts matched the shape of her nose.

He'd had a lot of time to study her. Once she had looked over his shoulder at his work, and a spoon-shaped breast had touched the side of his head. He could still feel it.

"I think boys ought to be taught by men," said Gloria.

Andy disagreed. He liked being with women, and he'd learned a lot from Maggie Thompson, not only about the shape of her breasts.

"Boys need men," said Gloria. "Otherwise they don't grow up to be masculine."

Andy groaned.

But girls could be taught by men or women, and she kept on in the same vein most of the way home.

"What are you doing tonight?" he asked again, as they turned into the lane where she lived.

"I'll have my tea."

He thought this was rather more hopeful. "What will you do then?"

"I'll do my piano practice."

"And then?"

"I could do some homework, but I could leave it." She paused. "I haven't got any that I've got to do for tomorrow."

Did he dare? Could he ask her to come out with him? His heart was pounding. Her gateway was just ahead. If he didn't ask her now, she would be through the gate and gone. He took the plunge. "Can I see you tonight?"

"What for?"

"I don't know . . . We could go for a ride."

She stopped, and got off her bike. She tossed back her dark hair, which had blown across her face when she was riding. "I'll think about it," she said.

"About half past seven."

"Maybe."

32

He rode home feeling jubilant.

"I'm just going out for a while," he called to his mum and dad in the sitting room.

"Have you done your homework?"

"I can finish it later."

He put on his cycle clips. They too embarrassed him. There was a lot about his appearance which embarrassed him. He had a pimple between the fold of his right-hand nostril and his cheek; he would have to keep the left-hand side of his face towards her. And he didn't like his short-back-and-sides haircut. He would like to grow his hair outrageously long.

He rode up to the lane. There was one car parked in it, and nobody about. He went to the end, where it narrowed into the original country lane, and back again.

Someone behind a window drew back a lace curtain and stared out. He wondered how long he could stay riding up and down without feeling too conspicuous. He felt sure she wouldn't come; it hadn't been a very definite arrangement.

He rode further down the lane into the countryside, and when he came back she had already left her house and was walking towards him. He rode straight at her at full speed, braking hard and skidding to the right at the last moment.

"Don't!" she said, wincing, and he felt silly, approaching her as he might have done one of his mates.

She had changed into slacks and a blouse. He thought she looked smashing, though perhaps everything was a bit too tight. He still wore his school blazer and flannels; he didn't have any other clothes apart from old ones for messing about in.

She looked so grown-up, it made him feel awkward. He couldn't think of anything to say, now that she was with him. He stayed on his bike.

He rode alongside her. On either side, the fields were separated from the lane by drainage ditches; there were no hedges and it all seemed very open. He said that a Cornish lane was usually between high banks, and she thought he was criticising Yorkshire again.

"I'm not saying it's better," he said. "I'm just saying it's different."

"You think it's better though."

"I didn't say so."

"That's all you think about," she said scornfully. "Everything has to be compared with Cornwall. Why don't you accept this place as it is? Or else go back if it's so wonderful."

"I don't think about it all the time." He thought about lots of other things, things he didn't dare tell her.

"Cornwall, Cornwall, Cornwall," she said. "That's all you talk about."

"I only said the hedges are different. Anyway, all you talk about is Bywaters School."

"It's better than any Cornish school."

"You don't really know what it's like."

"I know it better than you do."

"I *go* to it."

"I've known it for years. My dad went to it when it was only the old schoolhouse, and our Robert's been there as long as you have."

"It's not what you think it is."

She turned on him, her eyes blazing, like Cathy in *Wuthering Heights*. "I *know* what it's like."

"I could tell you a few things about Bywaters."

"I don't need *you* to tell me."

They came to a hump-backed bridge over a canal. He leaned his bike against the parapet, and they stood on the middle of the bridge, looking down at the water choked with reeds and sedge. They watched the dabchicks shunting about amongst the green weed.

"Go on, then," she said, after a while.

"Go on, what?" he asked. It flashed across his mind that she was telling him to put his arm around her, but that was wishful thinking.

34

"Tell me about Bywaters."

So he told her about the incident in the study at break. Perhaps he made the boy seem smaller and more frightened – he'd really been quite defiant – and altogether more of a pathetic victim, but on the whole it was a fair account. He enjoyed the way his story held her, and he made it last as long as possible, but before he had finished he got the impression that she was not getting the point. He was trying to show up Duckworth as a bully, and her eyes glowed more and more with approval.

"Oh, he's splendid," she said when he had finished.

"He's a swine."

"He's got to be like that, the head boy of Bywaters. It's for the good of the school. Oh, he's magnificent!"

"Don't be daft," he said. "He's unimaginative, he's narrow-minded, he's just like the school itself."

"You don't understand," she said. "It's his duty."

"He's dull and boring, he hasn't got an original idea in his head. He does what everyone has done before."

But Gloria wasn't listening.

"I'd do anything for him," she said. She sighed, and picked off some pieces of moss from the brick parapet and dropped them into the water. "It's not just because he's Gerry Duckworth, it's because he's head boy of the school. Whoever he is, there's something about being head boy: I'd do *anything* he asked me."

She didn't seem to realise that he was there. His intention in telling the story had been to destroy Duckworth; it had the opposite effect.

Gloria annoyed and irritated him, and yet he couldn't stop thinking about her. He wanted to be with her, even if it was only to argue and squabble.

He lay in bed dreaming about her. He remembered what she had said about putting the dog-rose in her bedroom, and the dog-rose was like a third eye through which he watched her. She stood in front of a wall covered with old

35

Founder's Day programmes and yellow rosettes, a prefect's cap with a golden tassel and a red and black scarf hanging from the picture rail; she undressed slowly.

She unzipped her slacks – he had noticed exactly where the zip went – and stepped out of them. She unbuttoned her blouse and slipped it off her shoulders. She stood in her brown knickers and white bra. She reached behind her back and undid the fastening . . .

Come off it, said the voice of reality. She probably throws her clothes off much as you do, and dives into bed.

But he kept going back to that moment when the fastener undid, running it over and over again like an old film.

English lessons took place in the library, and until the end of the term were shared between Maggie Thompson and Bomber Carrington. The group sat around one of the varnished wood tables, on padded library chairs, surrounded by shelves of books; the sun shone through the windows and the surface of the table gleamed smooth and golden. Insects were humming outside, and there was some distant birdsong. Andy thought he could hear the train on its way back to Barnsby.

Squadron-Leader Carrington returned the Chaucer essays, and as the bell had gone for break, dismissed the class. "I'd like you to wait a moment," he said to Andy, who thought he was going to tell him off for day-dreaming. It was about the only thing he ever got into trouble for.

"*Trewin*," he began, sliding his fingers along the smooth surface of the wood.

"Tre*win*," said Andy automatically.

"I admired your essay. You write very well. I suppose it's the Celtic strain in you."

"Thank you, sir."

"Have you thought what you are going to do?"

Andy watched his fingers, which were now circling round and round on the wood. The nails were white with the pressure. "I shall do my higher school certificate next summer."

The fingers stopped, and he looked up suddenly. "I think you ought to try for a Cambridge scholarship."

Andy had never thought about it; no one had suggested it before.

"You would go up in December and stay two or three days in college for interviews and examinations. It gives you a pleasant foretaste of Cambridge life. Would your parents be agreeable?"

"Yes, sir, I'm sure."

The fingers started pressing and smoothing again. "You write very well, *Trew*in –"

"Tre*win*, sir."

"– but you haven't read very much. Where do you get your books?"

"Well, there's the library."

"The library's very run down. I think you'd better . . . ah . . . borrow some of my books."

"Thank you very much, sir."

Carrington stood up. One side of his face was scarred and he had a big RAF moustache. He stared at the table, then held his hand stiff like the blade of a plane, and pressed it along the surface as far as he could reach. "Hm . . . smooth," he went. Andy supposed that was what five years in Bomber Command did for you.

He followed him through the dining hall and into the boarding part of the school, where Andy had never been before. They went upstairs and through a dormitory where the windows were wide open on each side, walking down the middle between two rows of beds covered with grey blankets. God, thought Andy, imagine having to sleep here!

They went along a dim corridor and he caught a glimpse of a row of toilets without doors. Even worse!

Carrington produced a key and unlocked a door, and

suddenly the corridor was bright with the light flooding in from the room.

"Come in, come in," said Carrington, and Andy followed him. He was in a very large room with tall windows in a big recess, giving a lot of light. There were bookshelves on every available wall space, a desk under the windows and some large, chintzy armchairs. It was what he imagined a room in a Cambridge college would be like. He hadn't imagined that anywhere in Bywaters could be so pleasant.

Carrington was putting down his books and taking off his gown, throwing it on to a chair and moving about in a way which seemed to signify that this was his home.

"Coffee," he said briskly, as though it was an order rather than an inquiry. He disappeared into a narrow room on one side, and Andy could hear water gushing into a kettle.

On the other side was a similar room, and through the open door he could see there was just space for a bed covered with a dark red eiderdown and above it a crucifix. When Carrington came back he went across and closed the door.

"Have a look at the books," he said. "I've only just unpacked them, I had to wait until the village carpenter could do the shelves. He's made quite a good job of them, don't you think?"

He was very friendly and chatty, not at all like a teacher now he was in his own room, and they pulled out books for Andy to read.

"What have you read of E. M. Forster?"

"*A Passage to India.*"

"You ought to read all the earlier ones. *Aspects of the Novel* is very useful. They are lectures he gave in Cambridge, some years before I went up. But I knew Morgan quite well."

Morgan? thought Andy. Then he remembered it was what the M. stood for in E. M. Forster. He was quite impressed that Carrington knew him well enough to call him by his middle name. He stored it up for his own use.

"Do you like D. H. Lawrence?"

"Very much," said Andy.

"They're all here," said Carrington, with a wave of the hand. "Even *Lady Chatterley's Lover* in the Paris edition; it's banned in this country. Vastly over-rated, of course. I shouldn't borrow it yet, but you could take it later on if you feel ready for it . . . What about Aldous Huxley?"

He made the coffee and they talked books, or rather he talked and Andy listened. Then he looked at his watch, and his manner suddenly changed.

"You'd better – ah – get back to your lessons."

He moved awkwardly across to the door, and Andy picked up his armful of books.

"Any time you like," he said vaguely, "just come up here, or get the key from me, and help yourself to . . . ah . . . what you want."

Break was just ending as Andy went back to the study with his load of books.

"Where've you been?" called Reg. "I made you some coffee."

"I've been in Carrington's room," said Andy.

This was greeted with knowing cries of "Oi, oi!" and "Watch it!"

"I borrowed some books."

"Don't make excuses. We know what you've been doing."

"'Bummer' Carrington," said one of the boarders.

Andy blushed. He didn't know what to say. He had never thought . . .

He was saved by the bell.

It was almost dark inside the church, with the evening light slanting through the stained-glass windows and casting large shadows behind the pillars. There was a dim electric glow over the keyboard of the organ, where Reg was practising the music for the next day's services. The door grated on its hinges, and Reg peered into the gloom beyond the small area of light, trying to see who was coming.

Andy called out to him. After visiting the library (and now he had all Carrington's books there was no real excuse to do that) he usually called in at St Wilfred's. There wasn't much else to do in Barnsby on a Saturday night.

When Reg heard his voice, he switched from hymns to jazz. He pulled out the volume, and the sound rang through the aisles. He perched on the edge of the organ bench, and his shoulders twisted and jerked to the rhythm.

Andy came and stood by him, watching his fingers striking the keyboard. They ended with a run and a crashing chord. The church was jumping with the music, the whole town would hear it.

The echo died away. Reg started playing a blues number, very softly. He was looking at Andy and grinning. Andy couldn't make out what it was about.

"I had one of the choir girls last night," he said, and his grin turned into a self-satisfied smirk.

"You didn't," said Andy.

"I did."

He changed the rhythm and began playing *In the Mood*, mouthing the words and twisting his shoulders, giving them an extra thrust on the last syllable of each line. "*Mr What d'ya call it, what ya doin' toni-ight?*"

"Who was she?"

"*Hope you're in the mood because I'm feeling jus' ri-ight.*"

"Go on, tell me."

"You know that girl I said was always hanging around after choir practice?"

"Vera?"

"Yeh." He gave his self-satisfied smirk again.

"You're making it up."

"She's not one of your Brown Cows," said Reg. "You're wasting your time there, you know. They'll never do it."

He got up and walked down the aisle to the second pew. Andy followed.

"That's where it happened," he said.

They stood looking down into the pew, a narrow pen or pit where the action had taken place. Reg rested his hand on the end of the dark wood, as though he owned it.

"It looks very uncomfortable," said Andy.

"We put down the kneeling mats."

"I see," said Andy.

But he couldn't really, he couldn't visualise it at all. He couldn't believe that a girl would take off her clothes and lie down in a pew. Not for Reg, or anyone else.

"Anyway, by the time we got that far," said Reg, "she couldn't care less about being comfortable."

They sat down; it seemed to please Reg to sprawl in the pew, the scene of his triumph. Andy didn't know whether to believe him or not. He didn't know, either, whether to believe what the boarders had said about Carrington.

"Reg," he said, "is it true about Bomber?"

"*Is it true . . . what they say . . . about Bomber,*" Reg went, with his head going from side to side.

"Honestly."

"That's what the boarders say."

But the boarders were an odd lot. They lived in a world of their own. They were cut off from all contact with the opposite sex and were bound to be interested in one another, despite all the sport and athletics the school provided to try to take their minds off it. They lived what seemed to Andy a very unnatural life. It was just the sort of thing they would say.

"What do *you* think?" he asked.

"Maybe he is, or maybe he isn't, I don't care," said Reg. "Why do you want to know?"

"I just wondered."

"Do you hope he's keen on you?"

"No," said Andy, indignantly; he didn't like the idea. "I didn't think someone who could become a Squadron-Leader would be like that."

"They're not all effeminate, you know."

"I can't imagine it."

"I can," said Reg. "If we were both boarders, I'd probably be keen on you."

"Bloody heck," said Andy. He grabbed a prayer mat and clouted Reg's head with it.

Reg threw up his arms to protect his face. He slid along the bench, picked up all the mats he could and pelted them at Andy.

But Andy still went for Reg's head, using the mat as a bludgeon. Reg grabbed his arms and they wrestled on the seat. They fell off on to the floor, and ended up with Reg sitting astride Andy, holding his arms to the ground above his head.

"You idiot," he said. He was rather mystified by Andy's sudden violence.

"Get off," said Andy.

"What did you do that for?"

"Let me get up, it's uncomfortable down here."

He made a sudden effort to free one arm, and pushed Reg backwards. They sat down again on the pew bench, and Reg dusted off the knees of his trousers.

"It must be awful to be a girl," said Andy. "Lying there and seeing you on top of her, your padded shoulders, your hair all long and greasy."

"She had her eyes closed."

"I don't blame her," said Andy. "Your face all distorted with passion and lust."

"She loved it," said Reg.

It was quite dark in the church by now. Andy sighed. "I can't remember a time when I didn't think about women," he said. "I remember when I was in the infant's class, we used to put out beds on the floor in the afternoon."

"Yes, we did the same," said Reg in sudden recognition.

"It was called *quiet time*, and we were supposed to go to sleep. I used to close my eyes and wait for the swish of the teacher's skirt. I'd time it just right and open my eyes, and I'd be looking up her silk stockings and her white thighs to her suspenders disappearing into a froth of material . . . She dressed well, did Miss Trevethan," said Andy dreamily.

On Monday, Gloria and Dorothy were waiting again outside the station, and this time Duckworth was on the train. As soon as she saw him Gloria gave up any pretence of talking to Andy. Her whole manner changed; she stood taller by the side of her bicycle, and threw back her shoulders. She seemed to tilt her face, so that it looked proud and interesting, and she threw her hair back over her shoulder. There was a tension about her whole body.

Andy noticed and appreciated it, even though it was meant for someone else. Duckworth fitted his feet into the toe straps of his racing bike, appearing for a moment very bow-legged as he did so, and pedalled off fast. He hadn't seen her.

"I must be off to the barber's, ready for next Friday," said Reg, tapping his pocket and giving Andy a wink.

Dorothy left soon after, and Andy left with Gloria. In the High Street they passed the butcher's shop, all green and white tiles, with the name "Butterfield" above the window. Her dad was scrubbing the counter, amongst the imitation parsley and the hanging paper bags printed with lambs. She gave him a wave.

"What did you do yesterday?" he asked, when they were out of the town. It was partly to make conversation, but he also wanted to know every detail of her life. He liked to think about what she was doing at any particular moment.

"We went to church, and then we had Sunday dinner, Yorkshire pudding –"

"Yorkshire pudding!"

"What's wrong with Yorkshire pudding?"

43

"The way Yorkshire people go on about it, you'd think it was something wonderful."

"Our mum makes lovely Yorkshire pudding."

"It's only flour and water, it doesn't even taste if you haven't got any gravy."

"It's better than Cornish pasties," she said. "They're only second-rate meat pies. Our dad wouldn't touch them."

"It was all the miner could afford."

She thought about it. "It's the same with Yorkshire pudding," she said. "It had to fill up the family before they ate the meat, because they couldn't afford a big joint."

It was a surprise conclusion, that they had something in common. They rode on in harmony.

"Are you coming out tonight?" he asked, when they came to her gate.

"No," she said. "I've got too much homework." Her mind seemed made up.

"I'll tell you something about Bywaters."

"What is it?"

"I'll tell you later." He wouldn't say any more.

"Well, I might come out for a while," she conceded.

The trouble was he now had to think of something to tell her. He had said it on the spur of the moment, thinking he could make something out of his visit to Carrington's rooms in the boarding part of the school. But he didn't particularly want to give her the impression that one of the masters was taking an interest in him.

He hurried through his homework and was on the canal bridge by half past seven. He sat on the parapet and waited. The swallows were diving low over the water; some of them were drinking as they flew, just flicking the surface with their beaks. He had seen them do the same on the river Fal (but he wouldn't tell Gloria that).

"I can't stay very long," she said as she came up to him. "I shouldn't have come really." She hadn't changed out of her brown school uniform.

"Let's walk on a bit," he said. The road beyond the canal led through cornfields to Houghton Hill, a mound which rose the best part of six feet above the surrounding plain. It was covered with trees, which gave it a little more height, and had the reputation of being a meeting place for lovers. "To go to Houghton Hill" was practically synonymous with making love.

"Let's stay here," she said. "I've only got a few minutes."

So they both sat on the parapet.

"What were you going to tell me?" she asked.

"What do you want to know?"

She looked suspicious. "You said you had something to tell me about Bywaters."

"There's a lot I could tell you."

She began to look angry. When she was angry she frowned, and her dark eyebrows almost met. "You haven't brought me out for nothing," she said. "If you're playing a trick on me, I won't see you again, *Trew*in."

"I could tell you about the boarders," he said. "Do you know what their latest craze is?"

"What?" she asked doubtfully.

"They set fire to one another's farts."

Dead silence.

"What did you say?"

Andy repeated it.

"I don't believe it," she said.

"They do," said Andy. "It's quite possible apparently, the gas is inflammable. Those who are really keen go on a special diet of beans to produce the right sort."

"You're making it up," said Gloria. She looked shocked, delighted and ready to hear more.

"Some of them are really expert, they have competitions to see who can shoot the furthest flame."

"Have you ever seen them?"

"No, they do it in the dormitory at night." Andy could picture them, running around with bushy tails of flame, like little devils.

45

Gloria laughed as she too imagined them. She was quite fascinated. "Do they burn themselves?" she asked.

"I suppose they have some mishaps," he said. "There's one boy who can play *God Save The King*." He had exhausted all he knew about it.

"Oh, I think that's funny," said Gloria, and as she laughed she rested her hand on Andy's arm. He was very aware of it there.

"Duckworth can't get over it. He's asked for a demonstration one lunch-time."

Gloria laughed delightedly.

"I think he means to try it himself." He had no idea whether he meant to or not, but it was a chance to put another nail into Duckworth's coffin. He couldn't imagine that the picture it conjured up, of Duckworth trying to set light to his own backside, would make him more attractive to Gloria.

"I like that," she said as she recovered from her laughter.

This was the moment. He turned to her, and with the feeling that he was acting in a play, said, "Gloria, will you go out with me?"

"I have come out with you."

"No, you know what I mean," he said. To be "going out" with someone meant to be their boyfriend or girlfriend, it meant going to the pictures with them and sitting in double seats at the back, it meant going to Houghton Hill. It was not at all the same as "coming out".

"I mean going out with me properly."

She didn't answer.

"I thought it was what they call it here, I don't know what they say back home."

"Back home!" she scoffed. "What do you mean, 'back home'?"

It was not what he would usually have said; it was his mother's expression. But he was feeling nervous, and it had slipped out.

"*This* is your home," she said crossly.

46

"Yes," he said. "Will you go to the pictures with me?" Though he didn't know how he could afford to pay for two.

She got up and looked at her watch. "I must be going," she said.

"But what's your answer?"

"I should like time to think it over," she said. "I'll give you an answer before the weekend."

Andy had thought that she might just possibly have said yes, though he really expected her to say no. Her answer surprised him. It seemed at first to be very mature, and he was rather impressed. Then it seemed to give too much importance to the whole thing. *I should like time to think it over.* The tone in which she said it echoed through his mind all week; it sounded like the heroine of a nineteenth century novel answering a proposal of marriage. The seriousness with which it was taken made him feel panicky.

Then later, as the week went on and the girls were never there outside the station waiting for them as they came off the train, he felt annoyed. He felt that he had been put into a foolish position, having to wait for an answer. He ought to be going out with her or not going out with her, without any fuss.

On Friday afternoon the girls were there. By now Andy felt quite anxious; it was as though he had started something much bigger than he could cope with. They both looked very serious.

He watched Duckworth riding away, bending low over his handlebars. He looked as though he was jet-propelled; Andy could imagine the flames shooting from his behind.

They soon broke up, and he rode home with Gloria without either of them saying much. They stopped under the oak tree at the end of the lane, their tyres resting on old brown leaves and acorns. The foliage was thick above their heads.

They sat on their bicycles. Gloria had one leg stretched

out to prop herself up; the light shone through the material of her dress and outlined the shape of her leg.

"Well?" he said, his mouth dry. He felt like a schoolboy brought up before one of the teachers.

"I've thought it over very carefully," she said in tones of great reasonableness. "I'm very flattered that you asked me, and I hope we shall always be good friends."

God, thought Andy. It was like something out of the problem page of his mother's magazine, on how to turn a boy down without hurting his feelings. She was enjoying the part.

"But I'm afraid the answer is no."

"Why?"

She twisted awkwardly on her saddle, and scuffed her foot on the ground. The carefully prepared part was over. "I don't want to go out with you."

Partly Andy felt that he should take it like a man, in true sporting fashion; he had tried and lost and it wasn't done to complain. But partly he felt furious that she should turn him down.

"Why?" he repeated.

"You've got to accept it."

"But you must have some reason. Why won't you go out with me?"

"I prefer Jeremy Duckworth."

"But you don't know him."

"He's older than you – you're too young."

"I'm not."

They argued over their ages, and established that she was in fact three months older than he was.

"What difference does that make?" he asked.

"I couldn't go out with anyone younger than me."

"Why not?" He thought she was afraid what her friends would say.

"It's not just a matter of age," she said. "I've said no."

He could see that she wouldn't change her mind. He dropped his bicycle against the tree, and leapt for the lowest branch. He swung from it, and working his feet against the trunk, got a leg over the bough. He sat up, and looked down at her. Her face was dappled with sunlight and shadow.

"I like you as a friend," she said.

He climbed higher. It was a good tree, a very ancient oak with almost a platform in the middle and stout branches going off in every direction.

"Are you coming up?" he called. He could only just see her now through the leaves.

She didn't answer.

He wished he was climbing with her, pulling her up from above, pushing her from below, her dress opening at the top and her skirt riding up around her waist, his knuckles pressing deep into her flesh, sometimes one of them ahead and sometimes the other, climbing higher and higher into the clouds.

"Where are you?" she called.

He couldn't see her at all now. He was high up, looking out towards Houghton Hill. He gave a Tarzan call.

He climbed down swiftly, hanging from the lowest bough by one arm, beating his chest with the other and calling, "Me Tarzan, you Jane." Then he dropped to the ground near her feet, with more of a jolt than he expected.

"Have you quite finished?" she said in a superior voice.

He was breathless after the climb, and felt rather foolish. What he had done had been childish, and yet he felt elated by it. "That was good," he said.

"Are you trying to show off or something?"

"Have you changed your mind?"

"No," she said emphatically. "I only waited to tell you one more thing. Another reason why I can't go out with you is that I wouldn't want to hurt Dorothy's feelings. She's keen on you."

"Dorothy?" he said in amazement.

"Yes, she'd like to go out with you."

"I'd rather go out with you."

49

"Will you though?"

Andy paused. He heard the sentence that had rung through his mind all week. *I should like time to think it over.* "All right," he said.

"Sanderson Road, half past two tomorrow," said Gloria.

They rode off in different directions.

He rode his bicycle down Sanderson Road as though he just happened to be going by. He wondered whether it was a hoax, planned by Gloria and Dorothy to make fun of him. Perhaps they would suddenly appear together from behind a privet hedge, pointing and giggling at him. Yet he knew really it was genuine.

It had been a rush to get there. They had school on Saturday mornings, to keep the boarders' minds off other things, and the train didn't get back until nearly two. He had hurried home, eaten the pasty which his mother had kept hot for him, and come back into town again.

He didn't know which house she lived in; he had never been there before. It was a cul-de-sac off the York road, a row of semis on each side. At the end he turned and rode back again.

Dorothy came out of a gate, wheeling her bicycle with the basket on the front handlebars, only now it wasn't full of school books. She must have been looking out for him. She wore a white dress with red dots on it; it had short sleeves and was slim fitting and quite long, coming below the knees. She mounted, with one foot still on the ground, and gave a push.

Andy turned in the road alongside her, his hands on the top of his dropped handlebars, and they said hullo. They rode along together.

They turned into the main road. She looked straight ahead, whilst he kept an eye on the traffic. If there were lorries and cars in both directions he put on a spurt and with a touch on the handlebars, turned in sharply ahead of her. Or else he dropped behind, and watched her pedalling

50

ahead of him, sitting very upright on the saddle, her legs turning rhythmically, her white dress flowing around and almost completely covering them. It flapped against the rear wheel, without getting caught in it. A lorry whooshed by.

He drew alongside again. "Where shall we go?" he asked.

"Where you like," she said.

They rode on for a while.

"Shall we go to Houghton Hill?" he asked.

"If you like."

They were out of the town now, and riding along a country road between hedges, with the flat countryside spreading to the horizon. There were vast fields of corn and potatoes, and they passed an air force station which was being dismantled, although there were still men in uniform amongst the huts.

They were approaching the hill from the opposite direction, and they came first to a heath. The sky overhead was dull, though it felt as though the sun was there behind the clouds.

"Shall we leave our bikes?" he asked.

"If you like," she said.

They hid them behind some bushes, because the airmen from the base would help themselves to any bikes that were left around. She took a white cardigan from her basket; there was an orange paperback lying underneath it.

"Let's walk," he said, with an attempt at briskness and gaiety which he didn't feel. He felt tense and anxious, and rather depressed. He wished he was with Gloria. He wished he could say something more original.

She didn't say anything.

They walked on across the heath, past the pond where he sometimes came to swim. It wasn't very deep, it only came up to your thighs. But you could float on it on a hot day. There were sedges on the bottom which made you wonder what you were stepping on. If you weren't careful you kicked up clouds of black mud which discoloured the water and took hours to settle again. He had once seen a grass snake swimming across the pond, like a capital S in the water.

If he had been with Gloria, he could have told her about this, but Dorothy was difficult to talk to. She walked on, slightly ahead of him, trailing her white cardigan first from one hand and then the other. It brushed across the heather.

Ahead of them was the dark line of the pines. They came to the bracken before the trees. She stopped, and looked back at him.

"Shall we make a camp?" he said, trying to be playful but it sounded childish. He thought of the oak tree yesterday; the platform at the base of all the spreading branches was a good camp.

"What do you mean?"

"Shall we sit down?"

"What for?"

"For a rest."

His heart sank. He was making hard work of it. He wished he was more debonair, sweeping her off her feet like the hero of a film. Though actually he didn't fancy her all that much.

"If you want to," she said, in that flat north-country voice of hers that she had used all day. He began to feel annoyed with her. Why didn't she say something different. It was her fault, she could try to make it more fun.

He crashed through the bracken, pushing the fronds away from his face, and she followed as best as she could. When they were completely surrounded, he stamped out a hollow. It was not much of a camp, and he felt stupid doing it. She stood and waited.

He sat down, and she sat next to him. It was very uncomfortable, the stalks of the bracken sticking into them, and it was damp where the green fronds had shaded the ground. He leaned over and kissed her on the lips. She made no response. He kissed her several times. Her eyes were open; they were a mauve-blue colour. He thought,

"There's another person behind those eyes." They were cold and distant, perhaps fearful, and yet only an inch or two from his own. He closed his own eyes, and she shifted slightly, moving her face away from him.

He felt even more annoyed with her. Why had she come with him if she didn't want him to kiss her? Why had she agreed to come into the ferns?

He put his hand on the top of her dress. He undid the buttons and slipped his hand inside. She was wearing a vest and no bra. She was very flat. He felt around both breasts, and then tried to reach under the cotton material. He pulled it up, easing it a little at a time; she did nothing to help or hinder him. After a while he had uncovered both breasts. He touched her nipples until they hardened.

She shifted slightly to make it easier for him. The fact that she did this filled him with delight; it was the most exciting thing that had happened. He looked up into her face.

Her eyes were filled with tears, and others – big glycerine drops – were rolling down her cheeks. They left a shiny track behind them. His excitement dissipated. He felt terrible. He didn't know what to do.

"What's the matter?" he asked.

She looked at him through her tears. "You're just like all the others," she said.

He had moved away, and now looked down at her where she lay beneath the bracken, her dress open to the waist, and her vest up around her neck and her breasts exposed. For a moment she seemed to him like a murder victim, discovered amongst the undergrowth by the police. He drew down her vest to cover her up.

He sat with his back to her. He pulled one of the stalks of bracken. It didn't break cleanly but splintered into many strands.

"Why shouldn't I be?" he asked slowly.

"I thought you'd be different."

He started stripping the fronds. "Well, I'm not," he said. He went on pulling the bracken to pieces.

"You just wanted to experiment with me."

"Isn't that what you wanted?"

"No."

"I'm sorry."

He heard her tucking in her clothes behind him, and when he turned round she had done up her buttons. She had wiped her eyes, though they were still red from crying.

He longed to get away. He stood up, and held out his hand to help her. They went back to their bikes and rode home in silence.

Never again, thought Andy. Reg was absolutely right about Brown Cows, they were far too complicated. He would have no more to do with them.

He resolved to get on with his work. Even though it was Saturday night, he went up to his room, took out his card-table and started to read.

He didn't want to go to St Wilfred's. Reg would want to boast about his prowess with the choir girl, giving a blow by blow account of the latest action and elaborating upon the details. He couldn't tell him what had really happened between him and Dorothy.

He looked out of the window, down to the railway track. It was the line they went on to Cornwall. They would be leaving soon, his mother had already packed for the holidays.

He couldn't get the events of the afternoon out of his mind. He wished it was Gloria who had gone with him to the hill. If it had been Gloria, he felt sure that everything would have been all right.

Next morning he got up at the usual time, even though it was the only day on which he could have a lie-in, and took a cup of tea to his parents. He rolled up his towel and swimming trunks, and stuffed them between his handle-bars and the light bracket. He rode into Barnsby and knocked up Reg. "Where were you last night?" Reg asked as soon as he opened the door.

"I was working."

"I wanted to tell you, Vera's coming this morning. She's bringing a friend for you."

"Thanks very much," said Andy. He had had enough of friends' arrangements.

The municipal baths were open from seven till nine o'clock. As they went through the swing doors, the familiar atmosphere greeted them: the magnified, echoing voices, the smell of chlorine, the condensation and steam, the wobbling light on the surface of the water. It was a place that Andy liked.

He changed in a cubicle, men on one side of the baths and women on the other. The duckboards were wet under his feet. He looked over the wooden door; the pool was already crowded.

He stepped outside and without any pause went straight to the edge and dived in. He felt the shock of cold, the water sliding along his limbs. He opened his eyes and saw the blurred, distorted world under the water, bodies like jelly and blobs of colour which were costumes. He weaved between the shapes, and then burst through the surface, shaking the water from his hair. His eyes smarted.

He did two quick lengths to warm up, and then had a look around. Reg was at the deep end, chatting to a curly-haired girl who was holding a green bathing cap. It looked as though she was waiting for Reg to go in the water before she put it on.

There were the usual people, the one-legged man who swam up and down, length after length without stopping. There were several fathers teaching their youngsters to swim. There were never any attractive girls at this time of day; it was too early for them, and the Sunday morning session attracted the serious swimmers.

He swam back up the pool to where Reg was standing, and climbed out.

"This is Vera," said Reg, and he gave Andy a wink.

Andy had formed a mental picture of a voluptuous, mature-looking girl, and Vera was just a kid in a green costume. He wouldn't have looked at her twice.

She had a friend with her called Doreen. She was wearing a pink costume made from a nubbly sort of material. She looked thin and undernourished. They were making a lot of fuss about entering the water. Vera stretched a foot over the edge to test the temperature with her toes, and withdrew it with a squeal.

"Heck, it's freezing," she said.

Reg threatened to push her in, and there was more squealing and holding on to one another. He put her down on the edge of the pool, her feet in the water. She was slipping in and screaming. The attendant blew his whistle; the blast was piercing in the enclosed, echoing space. Reg let go, and she dropped into the water. She came up spluttering.

"You wait," she said. "You just bloody wait."

She tried to splash him, but it only made a commotion around her. He ran up the steps to the top board, and dived.

The attendant with the whistle told her to put on her bathing cap. She sat on the steps and pulled it on. Her face looked round and silly without any hair.

The other girl went down to the shallow end and entered the water, one step at a time, very slowly. When the water reached the top of her legs she stayed there for ages, her hands in front of her scooping the water and splashing the bottom of her costume.

Andy dived in and swam up and down, alternating backstroke and butterfly. Eventually Doreen stepped right into the pool; she stood amongst all the little kids in their waterwings, wet up to the middle, hugging herself with her arms and shivering. Where the water stained her costume, it went a dark pink, and instead of clinging more tightly because of the wet it seem to sag.

He felt a bit sorry for her, and swam up to her. "Can you swim?" he asked.

She shook her head.

"Try floating," he said. "Get down in the water, you'll feel warmer. I'll support your head."

She went down a little, and jumped up. He couldn't persuade her and she seemed to resent his interference, so he swam away.

Later he saw Reg and Vera taking hold of her and forcing her under. The next time he saw her she was standing on the edge, dripping wet and shaking all over with the cold. She looked like a dog that had been in the water. She had her arm out and was pointing. She was calling. "Vera, fetch tow-el." Her accent made her sound like a little child.

The whistle blew and the water was cleared. It began to settle, and then a boy dived back in again, shattering the surface. The whistle went frantically and the boy got out. The surface of the water was strangely calm, and reflected light on to the ceilings of the cubicles.

Andy changed, and they all met on the steps outside. The girls were wearing thin dresses which clung to them; they still looked wet and their hair was in rats' tails. Doreen had a blue tinge around her mouth and her nose was sharp and pinched; she was shivering.

"Come on, let's run around t' park," said Reg. "Get you warmed up."

He tried to get her moving. She allowed herself to be pulled down the steps, and then she stood on the gravel of the path and wouldn't go any further.

"There's only one way," said Reg. "My dad once had three Wrens fall overboard into Arctic water. They wouldn't survive for more than thirty seconds in those conditions. There was only one thing he could do. He had to order them to strip off, and he rubbed them briskly with dry towels to restore their circulation."

"Anyway, that's what he told the court martial," said Andy. He could see where Reg got it from.

"No, he saved their lives," said Reg.

"You're not going to try and save my life," said Vera. "I wouldn't let you do that to me."

"You might have to."

And they went on and on, keeping the idea alive. Doreen stood miserably on the path, hugging the soggy lump of her towel. Andy didn't want to be left with her. He went and fetched his bike from the cycle racks, and sat waiting at the park gates. The sun was clear of the trees now, casting shadows across the new grass. It began to feel warm.

Reg joined him, waving goodbye to the girls. "*Adios, amigos,*" he shouted.

Andy felt mildly embarrassed for him. He thought that the gender was probably wrong too.

"What was the matter with you?" said Reg, when eventually they swept out into the road. "Why didn't you join us?"

"I didn't want to."

"They thought you were a right stuck-up twerp."

Andy shrugged.

"Will you come to Houghton Hill with us this afternoon?"

"No."

"Why not?"

"I don't want to."

"Heck, now I'm stuck with both of them," complained Reg. "It's not going to be much fun. What have you got against her?"

"I'm not keen on her, that's all."

"You're too fussy," said Reg. "She's not like your Brown Cows, she'll do it."

"I don't care."

"You've put me in a right spot now. I thought you'd be dead keen to come."

"I went there yesterday," said Andy. As soon as he had spoken, he regretted it.

Reg swerved across the road, nearly hitting him off his bike. "You sly bugger," he said. "Who was it?"

Andy could feel the smirk coming on to his face.

"Was it Gloria?"

He could hear the respect in his voice. Gloria was a class above Vera and Doreen, a real super-cow. He wished it was Gloria. He would have made a pact with the devil, or given ten years off his life, to have been able to say yes. "It was Dorothy," he said.

"Dorothy?" exclaimed Reg.

"Yes."

Reg grinned at him. "Was she all right?"

He didn't know what to say. He didn't want to brag like Reg, and know all the time that there was a vast gap between what he was boasting about and what really happened. "She was quite willing," he said.

"They all are," said Reg. "It stands to reason really, they want it as much as you do."

That was not the impression that Andy had. He thought that what they wanted was something rather different, though he didn't know what.

They reached Reg's house and wheeled their bikes around the back. His dad was away in the Navy, saving the lives of shivering Wrens; his mum was in the kitchen in her dressing-gown.

"Look at your hair, it's soaking wet," she scolded Reg as soon as they went in. "Come on, luv, let me give it a rub." She pulled down a towel from the airing rack, and used it briskly on his head. He pretended she was hurting him and made a lot of fuss, but submitted.

"Eh, what are you grinning at?" She turned to Andy as she finished. Andy was thinking of Chief Petty-Officer Willoughby and the three Wrens.

"Oh, nothing," he said.

"Do you want your turn, luv?" she asked. She had a warm, throaty voice. "Is that what you're waiting for?"

He sat down stiffly on the kitchen chair. She drew his head against her. He screwed up his eyes; he could feel the soft wool of her dressing-gown, the edge of a silk nightdress against his cheek, the movement of her breasts as she rubbed vigorously.

"There," she said, her hands dropping from his head after a last effort.

He lifted his face from the happy valley.

"You're a quiet one," she said softly. "You like that, don't you?"

"Yes."

"Come on then, one more rub."

She stood close to the chair, and drew him to her again. He could feel her belly pressed against his chest, the slipperiness of her nightdress.

She slowed down and raised his head. With the end of the towel bunched in her hand, she dried the front of his hair, pushing it back from his forehead. "I'm exhausted," she said at last.

Andy looked up. He felt dazed. He blew through his lips, making them vibrate; he didn't know why.

Laura Willoughby laughed. She made the boys a mug of hot chocolate each; it was the same as the cocoa that Andy had at home, but she always called it hot chocolate and it seemed extra delicious after a swim. They took their mugs into the front room, and Reg put his on the piano. She brought in a plate of home-made shortbread biscuits.

"I'm going to get dressed," she announced.

Reg started playing, a rather flashy piece by Rachmaninov which he had played in the last school concert. Andy lay back in his armchair, his scalp tingling from the rubbing with the towel; the hot chocolate warmed his inside and Laura Willoughby's last words echoed through his mind. He could imagine the *snap! crackle! pop!* of her getting dressed. He felt at ease.

He liked Reg's mum. She must have been at least thirty-five, even forty, but she was his idea of a real woman. He liked to listen to her and Reg talking together, more like lovers than mother and son. Reg could say anything to her, he was really cheeky sometimes.

He couldn't imagine talking to his own mum like that. Mrs Trewin wouldn't have approved of her. She would have said she was "common". Andy was intrigued by her.

After some jazz improvisation, it was time for Reg to go to St Wilfred's for the morning service. They left together. Andy always hoped that at the last moment Laura Willougby would call him back to help her mend a fuse or something, but he didn't think it was very likely.

As he rode home he saw the Butterfields driving in to Barnsby. They had a big old Humber car, and Mr Butterfield was sitting very upright at the wheel. Gloria was in the backseat, looking vacantly out of the window. She caught sight of him as they passed, and gave a regal wave.

Andy thought it was very funny.

Carrington was in a good mood. At the end of the lesson he began feeling the smoothness of the library table again. "Ah, *Trewi*n," he said.

"Tre*win*," said Andy.

"There was an envelope from Cambridge in the post this morning. Shall we . . . ah . . . have a look at it?"

So Andy followed him through the boarding part of the school, as he had done a week earlier, to the pleasant room lined with bookshelves. He was a bit on his guard, after what the other boys had said.

As he entered, he saw a cane lying across the small table in the centre of the room. Rather startled, he looked at Carrington, who had gone straight to the desk. Carrington turned and his eyes fell on it too.

"I'm afraid it's sometimes necessary," he said apologetically. "It keeps the younger boarders under control."

He picked it up and flung it on to his bed, closing the door of the cell-like room.

"It's the worst part of this job. I hate having to use it."

Andy thought he sounded hypocritical. "It must seem very dull after the Air Force," he said.

"There are some . . . ah . . . compensations," said Carrington, picking up a silver paper-knife from his desk. He slit open the large brown envelope, and took out a letter and some printed sheets. He seemed quite excited.

"I see George is back as director of studies," he said. "He was in intelligence during the war. You'll find him delightful."

They looked at the application form and at last year's scholarship paper. The questions were very general; they required a lot of reading, far more than Andy had done.

Carrington drew in his breath between his teeth. "That's a nasty one," he said. "Could you have a shot at it?"

"I wouldn't mind," said Andy.

So it was set for the week's work, and they picked others to answer in the holidays. Then there were the books that he needed to read for them. With his hand about to take a book from the shelf, Carrington suddenly froze. He turned his face, the side covered with livid scar tissue, towards Andy and stared. He looked as though some disaster had struck him.

"Latin," he said, in a voice of doom. "We'll come a cropper on Latin."

"I did three years at my other school."

"Thank God for that. You'll need to get it up to credit standard, it shouldn't be too difficult. If you don't get the credit, you can always try little-go." Andy didn't understand what he was talking about. "I could coach you after school."

The books piled up. "What did you think of Forster last week?"

"It's extraordinary," said Andy. "The school in *The Longest Journey*, it's this school exactly. The attitudes haven't changed at all and that was fifty years ago."

"We're still ruled by the philistines," Carrington agreed sadly.

The bell went, and he had forgotten all about coffee. Andy, too, had forgotten all about the rumours. He knew now what Carrington wanted from him, and it wasn't what the boarders said. He wanted a scholarship, so that through Andy he could relive his Cambridge days again.

He went to the library at the next opportunity and looked up "philistine". He found that besides being an inhabitant of south-west Palestine, it meant (without *cap*) a person of material outlook, indifferent to culture, i.e. Duckworth. It was a good word, and he stored it up. He chalked "Duckworth is a philistine" on one or two blackboards. It would worry Duckworth because he wouldn't be able to understand it.

He didn't expect to see the two girls after school, and they weren't at the station. However, he glanced cautiously along the High Street, thinking he might meet Dorothy by chance. He wanted to avoid her.

At tea-time he told his parents about the Cambridge scholarship. He hadn't mentioned it before. They looked at each other. "Are you good enough?" his mum asked.

Andy shrugged. "Carrington thinks so."

They asked a few more questions.

"You go ahead with it, boy," said his dad. "If you get a Cambridge degree you can do what you like. No one's going to push you around from pillar to post."

He went over again the story that was so familiar to them. How his office had been upgraded but he had not been upgraded with it. They brought in a chap from London, some blue-eyed boy, to run the office that he had been running for years, and packed *him* off to Yorkshire. That was how they treated a Cornishman.

His mum listened to it as though she was hearing it for the first time, making all the appropriate comments. Andy felt his dad had had a raw deal, but he had heard it so often that he wished he wouldn't keep on about it. He went on eating his egg and chips.

"They wouldn't dare do that to anyone with a Cambridge degree," his dad said. "We'll back you up, son."

They even let him off helping with the washing-up, and he went straight to his baize-topped card-table in the bedroom. A short while later, he heard someone ringing the front doorbell, which was unusual because they never had any visitors. He wondered if his parents would hear at the back of the house, and then he heard the door being unlocked.

His mother called up the stairs, "Andrew, it's for you."

Surprised, he came down and there framed in the doorway was Gloria. She looked apologetic, which was interesting because he'd never seen her look like that before. She was wearing a dress with a floral pattern.

"I'm sorry if I'm disturbing you," she said. "I wondered if you could help me with my homework. I've got some Chaucer to translate and I'm stuck."

She was asking a favour; her whole manner was different.

"I'll try," said Andy.

"Oh thanks." She was so grateful he couldn't believe it. She hadn't brought the books with her. Would he mind going round to her house?

"I won't be long, Mum," he shouted, and then turned to find that she was still standing right by him. He gave his dumpy little mum a hug and fetched his bike.

As he rode along he wondered what was happening. He didn't believe Gloria couldn't do her homework. Perhaps she had been talking to Dorothy during the course of the day. Perhaps Dorothy had built him up as a great lover. Gloria now wanted a share in him. *Trewin* the super-stud.

He remembered the real Tre*win*.

They weren't alone in the house. The big black Humber was on the drive, and Gloria introduced him to Mr and Mrs

Butterfield. They were both stout and comfortable. Mr Butterfield had a permanent amused smile, perhaps at the way life had treated him. He was supposed to have done very well on the black market during the war, and moved his family from the flat above the butcher's shop to the house at the edge of the town. He was also supposed to have a "kept woman" in the flat (this information came from Reg's mum one Sunday morning). Andy looked at him with curiosity. He was interested in a man of his accomplishments, but apart from the continual smile there didn't seem to be anything special about him.

"I've seen you ride past shop," he said to Andy, grinning broadly. He put his arm over Gloria's shoulder, and pulled her towards him.

"Shop," said Gloria scornfully, tossing her head.

"Aye, shop," he said. He seemed delighted that she dismissed his business, that she was too superior to have anything to do with it. "She's a right little madam," he said teasingly.

He seemed very proud and possessive of his busty daughter. He slid his hand down over her waist and on to her hips.

She played up to him, pouting and making eyes, a daddy's girl. He patted her bottom as she pulled away.

They went into the front room. There was a piano, a settee and easy chairs, and a bookcase containing a uniform edition of Dickens, in blue with gold lettering; the bookcase must have come with the set. Mrs Butterfield brought in cups of tea and biscuits. She called him "luv"; it was worlds away from the way Laura Willoughby said "luv". It was just motherly.

The Chaucer was dead easy. He rattled through it, and even Gloria couldn't put up a very convincing display of finding it difficult.

"Dorothy's very upset, you know," she said suddenly.

Oh no, thought Andy, feeling all his confidence draining out of his shoes. This was what she wanted him for, to go

65

over the events of Saturday afternoon. She had gone over it all with Dorothy at school. And of course, he could see now, they wouldn't talk about it like two boys would; they would discuss it in detail, exactly as it happened. He felt trapped.

He went on translating, even though they had reached the end of the passage set for her homework.

"I think you owe her an apology," said Gloria.

"I don't want to see her again."

"She doesn't want to see you again, after what happened," said Gloria. "But I think an apology is in order."

Andy felt out of his depth. He was annoyed at her interference, and he was annoyed by the way she phrased it. "What's it to do with you?" he asked.

"She's my friend."

"That's nothing to do with it."

"You've insulted her."

"I'm not going to apologise," said Andy. "She's the one who ought to apologise. She agreed to go with me, she made no objection – what did she expect to happen?"

Gloria stared into his eyes. "She wanted you to talk to her."

"Well, she didn't do much about it. Why didn't she say so?"

"Because she's shy, like you."

This, too, annoyed him and he thought of walking out, but he was held by her big brown eyes. "If that's all she wanted, she could talk to you," he said. "What did she want a boy for?"

"She thought you'd be interesting."

"Well, I wasn't."

"She likes books and she knows you read a lot. She wanted to know your opinions."

Andy groaned. "I don't like books, I just write essays about them. I haven't got any opinions."

"She wanted to talk about Virginia Woolf."

"I haven't read Virginia Woolf."

"Then you could have read some so that you could tell her what you thought."

Andy remembered the paperback in Dorothy's bicycle basket. If she imagined that he was going to sit down in the bracken and read Virginia Woolf aloud with her and then *discuss* it, she must be bonkers. It was more like school. It wasn't what he wanted at all.

"But you just went ahead with your own selfish objectives," said Gloria.

"I'd do it for *you*," he said, and nodded at the bookcase. "The complete Dickens if you like."

"You've been unfair to her."

"It was you I wanted to go out with."

"I told you, I'm not going out with you . . . But I don't mind seeing you."

"When?"

"You can call for me on Thursday if you like."

She had him on a string, thought Andy, as he cycled back to his work.

He rang the bell at the Butterfield's house, and the chimes sounded in the hall. He thought Gloria would have come straight out with him, but Mrs Butterfield came to the door and invited him in. He had to sit down in the living room and drink a cup of tea, and talk to Gloria's brother Robert.

Eventually Gloria appeared in blouse and slacks. "Oh, have I kept you waiting?" she asked, as though she didn't know he was there.

"That's all right."

"We won't be long, Mum," she said. "We just want to talk about Saturday."

He jumped. She hadn't told her mum all about him and Dorothy, surely?

"Founder's Day on Saturday," said Mrs Butterfield. Andy felt relieved.

They walked down the lane to the canal, and along the

tow-path. They heard some voices and splashing, and two boys in canoes came paddling down the open channel.

"Oh look!" she cried. She stood and watched them approach, red canvas canoes sliding through the water. "I love boats."

As they drew level, she called to the boys. "Are they yours?"

They dug in their paddles and the canoes slowed down. They drifted towards the bank. "What did ya say?"

"Are they yours?"

"Aye."

"Will you give us a go?"

The boys, who were about fourteen, looked at each other and smiled. "Naw," they said.

Gloria stood amongst the rushes on the very edge of the bank; Andy watched from the path. The boys dipped their paddles from time to time to maintain their position; the water dripped off the blades.

"Go on," she said, using all her charm.

"Naw."

"I'll pay you," she coaxed.

"What will you gi' us?"

"What would you like?"

The boys giggled.

"Come on," said Andy, wanting to get her away. He thought she was demeaning herself.

"I'll give you sixpence," she persisted. Her slacks were so tight that she could hardly squeeze her hand into a pocket, but she managed to produce the coin. She held it out, offering it to them.

"I'm going," said Andy, and he walked further along the towpath.

"It's all I've got," she said.

The boys laughed, and then suddenly like wild duck they took fright, and splashed away up the canal.

"Come back tomorrow," she called. "I'll give you a shilling." She caught up Andy. "I'd love a go in a canoe."

68

"I can't see you in a canoe," he said, trying to get even with her. "You wouldn't be able to squeeze into it. You can hardly get into your trousers."

She stood stock still. "Don't you talk to me like that," she said.

"And even if you got in, you're so top-heavy the canoe would capsize."

"You've got a cheek, Andy *Trew*in," she said. She glared at him, but he got the impression that she quite enjoyed it.

"Tre*win*," he said. "Why won't anybody say it right? The important bit is the *win*."

"It's proper daft."

"It means white, and *tre* means house. You wouldn't say white*house*, you'd say *white*house."

"If you say *white*house, you ought to say *Trew*in."

"No," exclaimed Andy. She had missed the point altogether.

They turned and walked back to the bridge. Gloria sat down on the parapet. "It's Founder's Day on Saturday," she said, echoing her mother.

"Worse luck," said Andy. It meant the loss of a whole Saturday afternoon and most of the evening. It meant wearing ATC uniform all day long. The only good thing about it was that the term ended the following week.

"We always go to Founder's Day," she said. She turned and looked into his eyes. "Will you do me a favour?"

"What will you gi' us?"

"I'll give you sixpence," she said, with a certain amount of self-mockery.

"I want all you've got," said Andy.

"I haven't got any more, honestly. You can see for yourself." She twisted so that he could feel in her pocket. He slid his hand in and felt around the constricted space, pressing against her leg.

"What do you want?" he asked.

"Will you introduce me to Gerry Duckworth?"

"No," he said. He took his hand away.

"Go on, please," she begged. "Andy Tre*win*."

"No."

"I'll be nice to you."

"What's the point?" said Andy. "If I get Duckworth to go out with you, you aren't going to go out with me."

"Andy Whitehouse," she said, mockingly. "What a name. It's a bit of a let–down, in't it?"

Andy rode to school on Founder's Day. There were no lessons, and there was no need to be there before the church parade. The road stretched straight to the horizon, and all along it as far as he could see were groups of cyclists. They disappeared into a shimmering haze.

It was already hot, and the thick material of his uniform chafed his legs. He had agreed to meet Reg, but somehow they had missed one another. Duckworth and Pugsley passed him, heads down, at full racing speed.

He passed under the railway and rode on leisurely between vast fields of sugar beet. The enormous blue sky, and flat countryside stretching without interruption to the horizon, gave him a sense of limitless possibilities. He had the feeling that everything was before him, that he was setting off into the immense unknown.

But it only led to Bywaters and Founder's Day. This was the climax of the school year, the chance for Bywaters to reaffirm and celebrate all it stood for. It began with the commemoration service at the village church.

They formed up in houses on the school playground. The boarders were all in charcoal-grey suits; they had big yellow daisies in their buttonholes. The hairdresser had visited the school the evening before, and they were all identically shorn. They had a scrubbed, gleaming look.

Old Man Harding came to inspect them. Out of the corner of his eye Andy saw a cyclist shooting down the side-road behind the trees. He wondered if it was Reg, but it wasn't. The Old Man saw him too.

"Come here, lad," he bellowed.

The boy leaned his bike against a tree, and came across the yard. Harding grinned wolfishly and strode towards him, his hand outstretched.

"Welcome to school," he said. "you're only twenty minutes late."

"I overslept," said the boy.

"Shake hands, lad," said the Old Man. "You've done well to get here."

Foolishly, the boy held out his hand.

Wham! The headmaster struck him across the side of the head with such force that it lifted him right off his feet. Then he crumpled, and stood there holding his head, about half the height that he was before.

Harding turned, and inspected the day-boys. They were a motley lot; some were in suits, some in blazers, and some like Andy in blue uniform. A few had added the traditional yellow flower. Last year he and Reg had worn dandelions; it seemed ages ago.

Reg still hadn't arrived. He must be skiving. There was no roll-call on Founder's Day, and he might get away with it. But the school was so small that anyone could easily be missed. Andy admired him; he wished he had done the same. But it wasn't so easy for him. There was nothing Reg wanted from the school; if the right job came up, he would leave. Andy needed a good testimonial when he applied for Cambridge.

Pugsley was the captain of Thwaite, as there were no upper sixth-formers left in the house. He arranged them according to size, in rows of three, the smallest at the front. Andy was in the back row.

The two boarding houses led off smartly. Thwaite came next.

"Thwaite House, atten. . .tion!" shouted Pugsley, his voice squeaking on the "shun". "Left . . . turn! By the right . . . quick . . . march!"

There was nothing more stupid than marching, Andy thought. It would never have occurred to him as a way of getting from one place to another. He could see no reason why they shouldn't just walk into church.

"Left, right, left, right," shouted Pugsley, running up and down the squad and enjoying his authority. "Get into step, *Trew*in."

Andy gave him a V sign.

They halted a little way back from the lych-gate of the church, under the yew trees. The boarding houses were still leading in, one row at a time. There were crowds of people lining the churchyard wall, watching the parade. It had been rehearsed many times.

The road cleared, and before Pugsley could bring his squad forward, a big black car pulled in and stopped right in front of the gate. It looked like the arrival of a wedding party.

Mrs Butterfield stepped out on the road side. Mr Butterfield was flustered; he saw the squad whose space he was taking and he called to his passengers to hurry up. Gloria alighted in front of the church.

A gasp went up from the crowd. She really did look like a bride. She swept her long dress out of the car, and paused for a moment. A red-faced Mr Butterfield swung the car away past Thwaite House.

God, thought Andy, Gloria must have gone mad. Why hadn't her mum and dad stopped her coming to Founder's Day in fancy dress? And then it dawned on him. This was the New Look. This was the latest post-war fashion, the return to almost ankle-length dresses. He had seen them in the *Daily Mirror*. But no one had yet seen them in these parts of Yorkshire. Gloria was the first to wear one.

She moved slowly towards the steps to the gate, walking like a model. The dress was very tight at the waist, emphasising her bust and hips, and it had a very low neckline. The back rows of Thwaite House started to cheer and wolf-whistle. It was sensational.

Duckworth came running forward, to find out why the parade had come to a stop.

"What's going on, Pugsley?" he demanded.

"Right," shouted Pugsley to gain attention, and some people thought he meant turn right and fall out, and began to break ranks and push towards the gate in a disorderly fashion, hoping to see more.

The noise continued as Gloria proceeded up the sunken path between the tombstones to the church door.

"My God," shouted Duckworth. "If the head hears this he'll be furious." Nothing enraged Old Man Harding more than wolf-whistles; they were the lowest depth of vulgarity.

The remains of Pugsley's squad shambled into church. Duckworth brought up his men, and as Andy went up the path he could hear behind him a lot of military commands and dressing by the right and shuffling of feet.

As soon as he was inside he looked for Gloria. All the visitors sat in the side aisles, and from his seat he could just see her profile. He studied it all through the lessons, and the long boring sermon, and the prayers for good old Bywaters, who founded the school in the seventeenth century.

He felt excited by the stir she had caused.

There were several cars parked on the sports field; most of them belonged to the parents of boarders. Amongst them was the black Humber, and in front of it the Butterfield family were having their picnic lunch. They had rugs spread on the grass, and in the middle was a big wicker hamper. There were matching plates and beakers, and they all had serviettes.

Andy was amused by the hamper; he had never seen one before, he thought they only existed in books like *The Wind in the Willows*.

"Are your mum and dad here?" asked Mrs Butterfield.

"No."

"What a shame they couldn't come." It had never occurred to them, it had never occurred to Andy; none of them felt much connection with Bywaters. "Sit down with us."

Andy sat down and opened his spam sandwiches. Mrs Butterfield kept offering him slices of pork pie and thick ham rolls, cold fried sausages and liver. He accepted a beaker of orange squash.

She kept on about Andy's parents and what they were missing, as though it worried her. There must be something wrong with parents who missed Founder's Day.

"Duckworth read the lesson beautifully," said Gloria. She was sitting on a tartan rug with her legs curled up beneath her; her skirt lay in a wide circle from which only her top half emerged, like Venus arising from the waves. Even her feet were covered.

"You could hear it," admitted Andy.

"Every word," said Gloria dreamily. She smoothed out a section of her carefully arranged skirt.

"He did a grand job," said Mr Butterfield.

Andy stared at Gloria's dress; it contained an enormous amount of material. Her dad grinned at him. "What do you think on't?" he asked.

"On what?"

Mr Butterfield jerked his head very slightly towards his daughter; he was very economical in all his movements. "New Look," he said.

"I don't know," said Andy. He thought she looked smashing.

"It won't catch on," said Mr Butterfield decisively. "Men won't like it."

"Huh," said Gloria. "All they want is to see a girl's legs."

He grinned slyly. "Aye, they like a bit of leg. That's human nature, in't it?"

Mrs Butterfield went to the car and fetched her box camera. She took a snap of them all sitting around the picnic hamper. Gloria stood up, shaking out the folds of her dress, and posed against the big, rounded bonnet of the car. Her mother took another snap.

74

Gloria twirled around, showing off the length of her skirt and the way it swung. "Do you like it?" she asked Andy.

"You could make three dresses out of all that material," he said, letting his Methodist ancestors speak for him.

She raised the hem a few inches. "You're like our dad, you just want to see more leg."

She continued provocatively raising and lowering the bottom of her skirt, tilting forward to look down at the slope of her ankles and her feet planted firmly on the turf in their high-heeled shoes. Then she glanced up at him. "Will you show me round?" she asked.

Everyone looked at her as they passed the other picnickers on the field. She enjoyed the impression she created, and Andy enjoyed being with her. She was conscious of her dress all the time.

"I bought it in Leeds," she said.

"Was it very expensive?"

"Our dad would have a fit if he knew."

They passed the marquee and went through the gardens, decorated with bunting strung between the chestnut trees, to the school buildings.

"Where is Jeremy Duckworth?" she asked.

"He's at the Founder's lunch with all the nobs."

"Is only the head boy invited?"

"Yes, it's Duckworth's big day."

He took her to the prefects' study. Pavel was sitting alone, playing chess with an imaginary opponent. Andy introduced him as the only genius in the school.

"And you," said Pavel courteously.

"The only *other* genius," corrected Andy.

It didn't impress Gloria; she could notice nothing but the study. She gazed around in awe. She must have often imagined the room, and now she seemed to be telling herself that she was actually in it, that it wasn't a dream.

It was strange to see her there, in such a masculine stronghold, amongst all the dusty books and sports gear, looking so feminine in her New Look dress. She was like a priestess in some temple. He felt he could worship her.

Her eyes wandered round the room, taking it all in. It was very squalid; there were old milk bottles and burnt saucepans, dirt and grime on all the ledges, junk everywhere.

"It's very small," she said, beginning to adjust her imagined picture to the reality. She looked along the books on the shelves. "Which is Duckworth's shelf?"

He pointed it out. She immediately noticed the gym shoe. "Is that the – ?" she asked.

Andy picked it up and dangled it by a lace in front of her. "You can hold it if you want to."

She shrank back, fascinated and repelled. She shook her head, and Andy flung it on to the shelf.

"Well, that's about all there is to see here," he said.

She left the study slowly, taking a last look around, storing up images for her dreams for the next few months.

He took her to the art room, where there was an exhibition of work. It was guarded by two fourth-formers, who said that they weren't allowed to let anyone in. He told them he was going to rearrange his drawings.

Andy wasn't very good at art, and had dropped the subject in the sixth form, but he had a knack for getting the likeness of a person. He had a series of cartoons in the exhibition; they were of teachers and prefects, and were based on jokes which would only make sense to anyone in the school. They were all on one side of a display stand, and he led Gloria to them. She stood and looked at them.

There was one of Carrington in uniform, with an exaggerated moustache. *I hear Carrington's got his wings*, said the caption.

She didn't show much response. "Did you do them?" she asked after a while. At last it had dawned on her. He had signed them all "Andy".

"Yes," he said, waiting for praise. But it didn't come.

She stared in silence at a drawing of the head boy as Donald Duck. "Is that meant to be Jeremy Duckworth?" she asked eventually.

"Yes."

"It doesn't look a bit like him."

She moved on to the next one. It showed Duckworth's big craggy head and humped shoulders; he was paddling a canoe, and it was labelled *The bore on the river Trent*.

"What does that mean?" she asked.

"Last Easter he led a canoe expedition on the river Trent," explained Andy. "The river Trent has a tidal wave which is called a 'bore'. The 'bore' on the river Trent, i.e. Duckworth. Get it?"

"Is that meant to be funny?"

"I thought it was quite good." He had to admit, though, that it didn't seem as funny now, after Gloria had killed it stone dead.

"You're quite bitchy, aren't you," she said impersonally. "You're more like a girl than a boy."

"I'm not," he said. "Look, I've got another idea. Can I draw you?"

"What for?"

"For the exhibition."

She was tempted; she liked the idea of anything which linked her with Bywaters. But she was still suspicious. "What are you going to say about me?"

He put all ideas about Brown Cows out of his mind. "It won't be nasty," he promised.

She swirled her skirts and adopted a pose; her raised chin made her look haughty and model-like. He found indian ink and a pen and the size of paper he wanted. He sat at the teacher's desk, and looked at her.

She stood in the sunlight which came streaming through the tall windows. It wasn't true what her dad said. The long skirt made her more mysterious, more exciting. It was an invitation to imagine her nylon-stockinged legs beneath the tent-like material. Amongst the mediocre drawings and paintings of the exhibition she looked radiant.

He started at the top, sketching her hair and face. Perhaps he could make a career of it, drawing strip cartoons like the author of *Jane*.

"They want a model at the art school," he said. Reg had told him. "To pose in the nude, two and sixpence an hour."

"I wouldn't do it for that."

"What would you do it for?"

"I wouldn't do it at all in public."

"Would you do it in private?"

"It depends."

"What does it depend on?"

"It depends on who it's for."

"Would you do it for me?"

"*No fear.*"

He came to the bust. His pen slowed down as he followed the shape, and his hands trembled a little. He felt as though he was actually touching her. He speeded up again as he came to the long, sweeping lines of the skirt. Then he sketched a car in the background, and it was finished.

She came and looked over his shoulder. "Not bad," she admitted.

The New Look comes to Bywaters, he wrote underneath, and pinned it to the screen.

The squadron marched on to the lawn, Sergeant Duckworth in the lead. When he had halted them, they once more went through all the business of dressing by the right. Andy pressed his chin to his right shoulder, held out his arm so that his finger tips just touched his neighbour's shoulder, and – although the distance was exactly right – shuffled his feet.

It always seemed quite ridiculous to him. The only thing you could do was to exaggerate the shuffling, which on a hard playground could produce a very satisfying noise. But it wouldn't work on grass.

78

"Eyes . . . front!" shouted Duckworth.

His head clicked back.

Duckworth marched to the end of each row and examined them for straightness. "Back a bit, number three . . . up a bit, number eight." When he was satisfied with the mechanical exactness of their placing, he stood them at ease. They waited for the inspection party.

Andy had already picked out Gloria, at the front of the audience. He could see she was watching Duckworth.

There was a stir at the entrance of the main school building, and Old Man Harding appeared, with the chairman of the governors and the clergyman who had preached the sermon and the commanding officer of the RAF base.

"Atten . . . tion!" shouted Duckworth. He always stood with his head jutting out from his shoulders. When he gave a command, it shot out even further and his Adam's apple leapt in his throat. But Gloria never saw anything ridiculous about him.

Duckworth went forward and saluted, his arm vibrating. It was like a scene from a film; she would be thrilled.

The inspection party started to move along the lines. Andy hoped no one would speak to him. He glazed his eyes as they approached, willing them away.

Even with his eyes unfocused, he could still see Gloria as a blur of light. Perhaps, after all, if he introduced her to Duckworth, she might see him as he really was. When she had seen the prefects' study, she had thought how small it was. A few words with Duckworth might cut him down to size, too.

Suddenly he felt a figure close to him, and fingers doing up the button of his breast pocket.

"What's your name?" asked the C.O.

"*Trew*in," said Andy, and he could have kicked himself. He had never said that before.

"Are you joining the RAF, *Trew*in?"

"Yes, sir," said Andy. But not if he could help it. If he got

79

a scholarship he would go straight to Cambridge, and not do his national service for years and years.

"Jolly good," said the C.O.

Duckworth was glaring darkly, annoyed that he had missed the undone button. Andy had let the side down again.

Duckworth's next appearance was as captain of the school cricket eleven, in the match against the parents. For this he changed for the third time that day. He had worn a double-breasted grey suit to read the first lesson at church, his sergeant's uniform for the ATC parade, and now he put on his white cricket flannels. It seemed to Andy, itching in his airforce blue, that it was all a conspiracy to impress Gloria.

He joined the Butterfields at the beginning of the match, but the talk was so much about the cricket team and whether Duckworth had scored thirty-six last year or the year before, that he walked away. He found Pavel, and they played a game of chess, lying in the uncut grass amongst all the meadow cranesbill in a far corner of the field.

He rejoined them at the interval for tea. They had opened their hamper again, and were eating buttered slices of Sally Lunn, rich fruit cake and cheese. But Gloria wanted a school tea, so she and Andy strolled across to the schoolhouse and joined the queue.

Tables were set out on the lawn with plates of sandwiches and cakes. Cups of tea were dispensed from a large urn by ladies in black dresses with frilly white aprons and lace caps.

They took their cups to a table under a chestnut tree at the edge of the lawn. As they were sitting down, Carrington approached wearing a blazer and flannels, with a silk scarf in his open-necked shirt. He was very apologetic for interrupting them, very deferential towards Gloria.

"I just wanted to say, I read your essay last night. I liked it. We'll talk about it on Monday."

"Thanks," said Andy.

He was pleased that Carrington liked his essay. He was

pleased too that Gloria heard his praise. He talked about Carrington and the Cambridge scholarship, but Gloria wasn't very interested.

"What was the score?" he asked to change the subject.

Her interest revived. The parents had won the toss and gone in first. They were all out for one hundred and fifty-six. The school were ninety-eight for five; Duckworth was fifty-four not out. The school had a chance of winning if the tail-enders held on.

It looked as though Duckworth would be the hero of the match. "I'd introduce you to him if I could," said Andy. "But it's not easy to get hold of him."

There was a special tea for the cricketers on the headmaster's lawn on the other side of the schoolhouse. He could catch glimpses of white through the bushes.

"That's all right," said Gloria. She seemed content to idolise him from a distance. It was Duckworth's day, and all the heroic roles he had played had swept her off her feet. She was more dazzled than ever.

There was a general movement towards the schoolhouse door. The cricket teams were coming. Gloria rushed with the others to the edge of the path.

Duckworth came through the door. He swung his bat under his arm, and strode down the aisle of people, looking to neither left nor right.

Interlude

A few days later Andy and his parents left for Cornwall. They always set off in a mood of excitement, and then as the long day went on they became bored and tired. Their spirits revived at Exeter. They were nearly home.

The track passed along the side of the estuary, and then by the sea itself. The train plunged into tunnels in the red cliffs and out on to the sea wall. Sometimes in winter the announcer at Exeter Station would warn people to close the carriage windows because of rough seas, and in the dark the spray would lash against the glass.

But on a late afternoon in summer the Channel was still, and only the smoke beat against the windows as the train entered a tunnel. The sea was blue; there were ships on the horizon and even people on the beaches now that the coastal defences had been dismantled.

At Plymouth their excitement mounted. Soon the train was creeping over Brunel's iron bridge, nearly one hundred years old, and they were across the Tamar and in Cornwall; further down the train someone called "Oggy, oggy, oggy", and a carriage full of sailors answered with a great cry of "Oi, oi, oi". They began singing *Camborne Hill*.

Andy and his mother and father looked at one another and smiled and were happy to be back. Andy felt it as much as his parents. They began to get their cases down from the racks, and put all their belongings together near the doorway. They were standing long before the train slowed down to cross the viaduct into Truro station.

There were his Uncle Jack and Aunt Mary waiting for them, waving as they came through the barrier, and then they were hugging and embracing, as though they were emigrants back from Australia, South Africa or California, instead of just Yorkshire. His uncle drove them to the cottage overlooking the river, and as soon as they were there it seemed as though they had never been away. Yorkshire ceased to exist.

After a meal, he went down to the water's edge. It was a very quiet evening; the tide was nearly in, and everything was still. A few small boats rode on their moorings, and the launch that his uncle used in his work as a river pilot swung gently in the current. The sky was still light behind the wooded slopes of the opposite bank, but the water was dark. Downriver, a curlew called.

In the morning he watched his uncle in the workshop. Uncle Jack had acquired a big American marine engine which he was overhauling. He took it to pieces very methodically, working slowly and patiently. He probed and explored, reasoning things out. He knew he would win in the end.

As he worked, with Andy and his dad lending a hand, he talked about the river. He said that cargoes from ships sunk in the war were still being washed ashore; he still went beachcombing. In the last storm he had seen a dinghy drifting. He had chased after it in the wind and rain, and tied it up below the cottage. He thought at least the owner would thank him, but a few days later he turned up and accused him of stealing it.

The next day they went downriver to bring up a Scandinavian timber boat on the tide. It was a big boat, and the deep channel was very narrow in places; his uncle had to know the river exactly to take it through. He enjoyed being with his uncle and the other men, the way they talked and the way they set about their work and used their skill.

He looked up his old friends; they had been together in Miss Trevethan's class at the village school. He watched them putting their mackerel lines into a boat.

"Hullo, Trewin, fancy seeing you. What are you doing these days?"

But nothing came of it. He had been away too long and they had grown apart.

He thought how strange it was, that a decision taken in an office in London, could make such a difference to his life. If his father had been promoted, he would still be living here, and William Hooper and Luther Mitchell would still be his best friends. He didn't join them, but watched them push the bows off from the gravel beach and row downriver.

All his parents' friends were here. But for the first time he felt that part of himself belonged in Yorkshire.

They walked along the cliffs one afternoon. The path was high up above the sea, through low gorse and heather. The sea was blue-green, with white breakers. There were miles of coastline in sight, with headlands and islands. They came to some old mine-buildings, right on the edge of the cliff.

He thought of Gloria, on holiday near Whitby. The Butterfields were going to stay on the farm where they had always spent their holidays until the second year of the war; Gloria was very excited about it. "Why do you always go to Cornwall?" she said. "Why don't you see more of Yorkshire while you're here? You could go to the moors, or the dales, or the sea."

The first week seemed to last for ever. On Saturday he suddenly thought, "This time last week I was at Founder's Day." It seemed a different world, a lifetime away. In the second week time returned, and began to speed up.

His father would have to go back in a few days. He was very gloomy about it. He thought he would never be transferred to Cornwall. If he were, he would never be able to afford a house. Whenever they went by their old house, which was just down the road, Mr Trewin said that he should never have sold it. It had been a great mistake; he had practically given it away in wartime. Now prices were going up, and he wouldn't make much on the house in Yorkshire.

Once he had gone, it seemed as though the official holiday was over. Andy tried to give more time to his scholarship work. His room had a sloping ceiling, and a low window which looked on to the river. He sat in the window seat and read. The light came bright off the water. Boats passed up and down; the wash of a small tanker lapped against the walls of the cottage.

There were wild plum trees growing all along the banks; at high tide his mum and aunt Mary took out a rowing boat. The best fruit could only be reached from the river. He could hear the splash of the oars, and their voices carried clear across the water. They laughed a lot, and shrieked like schoolgirls when they reached for the plums and the boat wobbled unsteadily. Afterwards they would bottle some of the fruit, making the rest into jam. They would take several jars back to Yorkshire.

It was the prawning season, and at low tide men waded along the water's edge pushing large nets in front of them. The river was full of fish, mullet, bass and pollack, and one evening the surface of the water was alive with a shoal of mackerel, jumping and splashing.

There were always distractions. On Friday he went to a dance in the village hall, and danced a few times with a mousey-haired girl. Without saying anything, she seemed to take it for granted that he would walk her home.

They stopped by her gate. The house was up a long garden path, and all the windows were dark. There was a tree by the gate, and she leaned against the trunk as though she had done it many times before.

A few lights shone from the village, and were reflected in the water. She kissed in a very practised sort of way, except that in her eagerness he could feel her teeth behind her lips. Her dress had three buttons at the neck, which made a very small opening. He could only get his hand inside if he stuck his elbow up in the air, right across her face. Even then, he thought he heard something tear.

He slid his fingers down. She was wearing a vest and no bra. Her breast – he could only reach one – was soft in his hand, like dough.

He had cramp in his arm. He tried to take his hand out, and there was another splitting sound.

"Linda!" shouted a woman's voice, unmistakably a mother's. The door had opened, and yellow electric light was flooding down the garden path and into the tree above them.

Linda straightened her clothes, and hurried up to the house. She disappeared inside to the accompaniment of a lot of scolding noises and a slap or two. The door slammed.

Everything was very quiet. He walked back along the riverside and thought about Dorothy and Linda. Both of them hadn't even worn bras, they wore vests like kids. It seemed to him that girls who had small breasts were much more likely to let you feel them than girls who had big breasts.

He made up his mind. In the new school year he would try really hard to get Gloria to go out with him.

On the last morning of the holidays he went down to the river, straight after breakfast. The water was covered with a wispy mist about a foot above the surface. It was very eerie; it seemed to move downstream very fast, swirling around the hulls of the boats. He stood and watched until it was time to go for the train.

Part Two

The platform at Barnsby station was crowded with new boys. They stood out because they looked so young and small, as though they should still be at primary school. They wore brand-new blazers which were generally too big for them, or long navy-blue raincoats; the satchels they carried seemed vast and shiny. They were a bit over-awed.

The older boys looked them over as though they were cattle. "Aren't they small!" they said. "Aren't they tichy!" It made them feel ten feet tall.

The train came in slowly from its siding, and everyone got on board. Andy collected the *Daily Express* for the library, and saved a compartment for the prefects. He supposed he would be a prefect now he was in the upper sixth, but he didn't intend to behave any differently.

Reg arrived and started talking about his holidays. To make some money, he had been to an agricultural camp, picking potatoes. He said the Land Girls were terrific.

Pugsley arrived late, but before the train started to move. He walked the length of the two carriages, peering into the compartments, and then returned to Andy and Reg. As they left the station, he dropped the window and leaned out. "Get your heads in!" he bawled. "Right, Parkyn, come to the study at break."

They settled down to the journey. It began to seem as though the holidays had never been. The six weeks in

Cornwall ceased to exist, and it felt as though they had continued to travel to school daily.

Pugsley saw everyone off the train and down the slope. He snapped off a whippy length of stick. "I feel like a mush," he said.

"Oh no," said Andy and Reg. Not on the first day of term.

"We'll be late otherwise."

"So what?"

"It takes longer this way."

On the first and last days of term the train boys always took a different route to school; they turned right and the road meandered through the countryside, passing an orchard before coming back into the village. As it was longer, they often ran.

"They'll have to wait for us."

Pugsley looked displeased; he didn't want to drive a mush on his own, without their support. He slashed the stick against his own trouser leg. As soon as one Duckworth went, thought Andy, another took his place. Pugsley was a boy in the same mould. He had been groomed by Duckworth to be his successor.

They weren't any later for assembly. This took place in the village church on three mornings a week, and in the new school on the other three, when the partitions were withdrawn between three classrooms. For special occasions, such as the first day of the school year, or the public beating that Old Man Harding gave some unfortunate lad about once a term in order to encourage the others, assembly was held in the old schoolhouse.

This was a large, chapel-like building open to the rafters, with an arched window in one end. It was fitted out as a gym, with wall bars, climbing ropes and beams. It was also used as an examinations hall.

They all filed in. Andy and Reg leaned against a gym horse at the back. Pugsley waited at the door, and as soon as he saw the staff leaving the new school he shouted "Quiet!" and glared around, looking for anyone who dared to speak.

The teachers walked up the middle and stood beneath the window. There was a suitable pause.

"Stand!" shouted Pugsley, and although everyone was standing already, they straightened their shoulders and stood taller. Even Andy and Reg eased their backs off the horse.

The hefty figure of Old Man Harding, in a black suit and with his black gown flapping, swept through the assembly to the front. The music master played a few bars of introduction, and they sang the hymn: *O God our help in ages past*. The Old Man thanked God for the holidays that were past, and prayed for strength for the year to come. He spoke of the need to work hard and play hard.

Then he began the lists. Andy could never understand why he had to read through the list of every boy in every form, but he always did. It was very long and very boring, and could only interest the few who thought they might have to repeat a year. The Old Man cleared his throat, eyed the assembly and began.

"School officers for the new year. Head boy: *Trew*in, A. Deputy head boy . . ."

Andy couldn't believe his ears. Nor, it seemed, could a lot of others. There was a buzz around the hall.

"I'll repeat that," said the Old Man, in a tone which immediately stopped the murmers. "Head boy: *Trew*in, A. Deputy head boy: Pugsley, P. Prefects . . ."

There must be some mistake, thought Andy. It had never occurred to him that he would be appointed. Everybody knew that Pugsley would be head boy; it was taken for granted.

He glanced across at Pugsley, P, standing just inside the door. Pugsley was trying to look as though nothing had happened. He stared straight ahead, listening to who were monitors in the lower sixth. It must have been a shock to him. He'd feel he'd been made a fool, acting as head boy and then finding he wasn't. He looked stunned.

Andy felt stunned too. The reality of it was beginning to sink in. He thought of all the things that would be expected of him. He didn't want to do any of it. It wasn't an honour, it was a bore. Pugsley could have it.

The assembly ended, and the staff filed out. As soon as they had gone, everyone started talking. Reg clapped him on the shoulder. "Congratulations!" he said.

"I don't want it," hissed Andy.

Pugsley had disappeared.

The noise grew, and everyone was pushing to get through the door. It became more and more of a scrimmage. It was Andy's responsibility.

"Wait!" he shouted. "Keep back, you'll get through if you wait a moment." He dived in and started pulling and pushing boys aside.

They were good-humoured and it worked, more or less. If Duckworth had been there, it wouldn't even have started.

Andy saw the last of them through the door. He had no pleasure in pushing people about; it didn't thrill him at all. It made him feel slightly sick.

And he was in for a year of it. Each day from the moment he reached the station, all through the journey and the walk to school – he'd do away with mushes, that was certain – and at assemblies in the church or in the classrooms, during break and all through lunch-time until he got back to Barnsby in the evening, it would be his responsibility.

He couldn't understand why the Old Man had done it. He was younger than some of the others, and he didn't belong to the school in the same way. He was an outsider; they wouldn't take it from him.

It was all a big mistake.

At break when he came in he heard Pugsley talking to Nobby Clark. "It was that bloody shambles last Founder's Day," he was saying. "That's what did it."

It didn't seem to Andy sufficient reason for not making

Pugsley head boy. He would have been very good at the job, another Duckworth. That's what everyone thought.

He took the coffee that had been made for him, and stood in front of the empty fireplace. Pugsley avoided looking at him.

There was a knock at the door. It was Parkyn. He stood in front of Andy: a boy from the middle of the school, with silky auburn hair and freckles on his face. "What do you want?"

"Pugsley sent for me."

"Well, there he is," said Andy, indicating with his arm.

"You've got to deal with him now," said Pugsley. "That's your job." Nobby Clark picked up Duckworth's old gym shoe and held it out to him.

Everybody was watching, waiting to see what he did. He felt that he was in some sort of arena, a gladiator to provide a spectacle. They wanted to see how he would shape.

It was the moment that would make or break him. He could beat the boy and if he made him cringe – and Parkyn didn't look as though he would be too difficult to hurt, in fact he suddenly saw why Pugsley had chosen him – he would be accepted as Duckworth's successor. There would be no more trouble from Pugsley. But he would have set out on the road to become another little Duckworth himself.

If he didn't beat him, he would have Pugsley leading most of the other prefects against him for the rest of the year. All of these considerations passed rapidly through his mind, but in the end he knew that he couldn't do it. He couldn't take a gym shoe and hit somebody else with it across the arse. He simply found it ridiculous.

They were all hushed, waiting for him.

"What were you sent for?" he asked.

"For having my head out of the window."

"Well, I didn't see you," said Andy. "But make sure I don't see you tomorrow, or you'll be back here again."

"Thanks," said Parkyn with a sigh of relief. He left as quickly as he could.

"Hmm," went Pugsley, as though they had started off on a very slippery slope indeed. Perhaps they had.

He had thought of Gloria, even as the Old Man had been reading out the list of names. She believed there was something special about being head boy. It didn't matter who it was, she had said. She'd do anything for him. *Anything.*

And now he was head boy. The thought of Gloria pushed all the disadvantages into the back of his mind. It would be worth it.

He didn't tell his parents, because he didn't really believe it was true. He hurried through his tea, and cycled to Gloria's. Her mum was full of congratulations; she obviously thought it was a great honour. He could hear Gloria practising in the front room. He wondered if she would be just as impressed.

Mrs Butterfield kept him a long time, talking about his holiday in Cornwall and their holiday in Whitby. When he went in to the front room, Gloria continued playing. It was a Beethoven sonata; it looked very difficult and she frowned at her mistakes. He sat down and listened; he didn't think she was as good as Reg.

She stopped playing and flicked over some pages.

"Have you heard?" asked Andy.

"Heard what?"

"I'm head boy." He hadn't wanted to say it; he had wanted her to say it.

"Oh, that."

"Well, what do you think about it?"

"I think it's a great mistake." She swung round on the piano stool to face him. "They ought to have chosen Peter Pugsley."

It was all going wrong. She ought by now to have been kneeling on the carpet before him, kissing his feet.

"They ought never to have chosen you," she went on. "They must be mad, it'll be an absolute disaster."

She swung back to the keyboard. In her winter school uniform she was all in brown: brown jumper and skirt, brown woollen stockings and brown shoes. She had a large white grip holding back her dark brown hair. She looked more lovely than he had remembered.

He sat reading the *Daily Express*. The engine hooted and got up steam. If any of the boys wanted to look out of the window and get their heads knocked off, that was their decision; they were old enough to make up their own minds. It was unlikely to happen anyway.

He wondered why it was such an attraction. If no one shouted to them to get their heads in, would they not bother to look out? Or would they hang out more and more until there was an accident? But if any were being pushed or held out . . .

He got up and dropped the window. The train was just beginning to move. He leaned out, feeling the air against his face. Heads and shoulders were hanging out all along the line. "Get your heads in," he bawled. They disappeared as if by magic.

Get your heads in, Quiet, Stand, Atten . . . tion! He hated all this shouting. Anyway, he wasn't going to do it. He had made up his mind to resign. And while he was about it, he would resign from the ATC as well.

After assembly he went to see the Old Man. He asked Reg to give a message to Carrington explaining his absence, and he asked Pavel to show him the way. It seemed extraordinary not to know where the headmaster's study was, but most day-boys never visited it. Andy had been there once, on the day he arrived at the school in the middle of a term, but he couldn't have found it again. It was in the Old Man's private house, attached to the boarding part of the school, at the end of a maze of long, dark passages.

Andy stood in front of the door. It might have been a bedroom for all he knew. He felt the enormity of what he was doing. Nobody at Bywaters ever questioned anything.

If you were appointed, you carried out your job to the best of your ability. If you weren't, you didn't complain. You accepted everything.

He knocked at the door.

"Come in," called Harding.

Andy went in. The Old Man was standing in front of the tall Georgian window looking out into the garden. It was like being in a country vicarage; it seemed miles away from the school. At a desk in the corner was the new secretary, one of the girls from the grammar school; she was either Beverley, or Valerie, the prettier one at sports day.

"About being head boy," he began hesitantly.

"Yes," said the Old Man, turning around.

"I'd like to talk about it." After all, he thought, it wasn't unreasonable to talk about it. Though at Bywaters the headmaster never discussed with the head boy what his role was. He was expected to carry on like his predecessor.

"What is it?"

"I don't want to accept it."

The Old Man raised his thick, black eyebrows; it was a well-known danger signal in his scripture lessons. It was usually done in mock surprise, but this looked genuine enough. "Why not?" he asked sharply.

"I don't think I'm the right person."

"We think you are."

"But I've come from outside." It was his father's expression; the Londoner who had taken his job in Cornwall had "come from outside".

"That makes no difference, lad."

"I think Pugsley would be much better."

The Old Man sat down at his desk, with a look of resignation on his face; he'd rather be doing something else. "Sit down, lad," he said.

Andy sat on a chair in front of the large desk. Out of the corner of his eye he saw Valerie – or Beverley – pretending to be busy with the post, listening to all that was said.

Harding picked up his pipe, and started to poke around in it with a metal spike. "Pugsley would do a good job," he said, "but he wouldn't gain from the experience. We thought you might."

Andy was suspicious of anything that was supposed to be for his own good. "It's unfair to Pugsley," he said. "He expected to be chosen."

"That'll do him no harm."

"Couldn't you have an election?" asked Andy. If it was put to the vote, the school would choose Pugsley, just as Gloria had.

"Democracy, eh?" said the Old Man. "I don't believe in it, least of all in school. It always leads to the wrong choice. Look what happened to Churchill in the election."

"Then how do you choose?"

"The staff make recommendations. I listen to them and then I make up my own mind."

"But why choose me?"

"Some of the masters feel it's time for a change. They thought you might have a different approach to the job."

"I don't want the job," said Andy.

"A lot of people have put their trust in you," said the Old Man. "Carrington particularly thinks you'll have some new ideas. You can't let them down."

So it was all Carrington's fault. But what they wanted was still so vague. "What sort of head boy do you expect me to be?"

"That's up to you, lad," said Harding.

"I can't be like Duckworth," he said.

"You'll have to find your own way."

"Duckworth used to beat a lot."

"Did he?" exclaimed the Old Man. "I had no idea." He was obviously lying. "He had no right to do that, of course."

"I see," said Andy.

"This school's done a lot for you, *Trew*in. Now's your chance to give something in return. It's up to you, to make what you want of it. And don't forget, it'll look very good on your Cambridge application."

"Yes, sir," said Andy. It was clear the interview was over, and he left.

The moment he was outside he realised what he had done. He had gone in intending to resign, and he had come out agreeing to accept. The Old Man had talked him into it.

He couldn't understand, it was unlike old Harding to want any change. Perhaps he appointed Andy, hoping that he would make a mess of it. Then next year he could say to the teachers back from the war, "Well, we tried out some new ideas and they didn't work. Let's stick to the old way now." And the Duckworths and the Pugsleys would rule forever. That might be a good reason for having a go at it.

It wasn't until he fetched his books from the study that he remembered he hadn't said anything at all about the ATC.

There was a long queue outside the study door at break, stretching way back into the common room. "What's going on?" asked Andy, as he went in, though he had a pretty good idea.

"They're to see you," said Pugsley.

"What's it all about?"

Pugsley had booked two boys for talking in church, Nobby Clark had a boy for not wearing a cap and another without a tie, Sowerby had a boy for cheek; Wrightson, Painter and Harris, every day-boy prefect except Reg Willoughby, had sent someone to the study.

Andy went to the door and spoke to the queue. "Go into room one and wait there until I come." They all went quietly.

He could see how easily you could become a Duckworth; you could even begin to enjoy it.

He went back to stand in front of the empty grate. "Will you close the door?" They were waiting for him to speak.

He looked around. He would much rather be at the back, criticising what was being said. He could easily churn out the script of a Duckworth speech. He could hear phrases of it now, about all pulling together and not having any slackness.

"I've had a talk with the Old Man," he said. This in itself was quite startling; they were all silent. "I wanted to resign, but he wouldn't have it. He wants some changes."

"What, Old Man Harding?" said Sowerby, unbelieving.

"He's under pressure from the staff."

"From Carrington, you mean."

"And others. Duckworth went too far. He had no right to beat anyone."

There was an outcry. "The head boy has always done it."

"Harding didn't know about it."

"Of course he did, everyone knew. It might not have been official, but he turned a blind eye to it."

"Well, now it's stopped," said Andy. He picked up the gym shoe which had been left on the mantelpiece, and dropped it in the waste-paper basket. "That's it, it's finished with."

Several voices rose in protest. "What did you say anything for?" asked Pugsley. "If you ask him outright he's got to say no, but if you hadn't said anything it could have gone on the same."

"It's not going on the same," said Andy. "From now on, you don't send people to the study for the head boy to deal with. If you see something wrong, you deal with it yourself."

"But how?" they wanted to know.

"You've got to persuade them." He tried to argue that this way they had much more status, but they weren't convinced.

"The whole place will fall to pieces," said Pugsley. "I'd give it two weeks at the most."

The Open Door Theatre was presenting two plays at the girls' grammar school, a different play on two consecutive evenings. It was a good reason for going to see Gloria.

When he went into the front room she was on the settee, reading. And she was wearing glasses.

"I didn't know you wore glasses," he said, surprised.

She snatched them off quickly. "Sometimes," she said.

"Put them on again," he asked. He liked them; they made her look very studious. But she thought he was laughing at her, and put them away in their case.

He was amused that she didn't want him to see her in glasses, and rather pleased. It was something that he hadn't known about her before. He sat down next to her on the settee. "I've agreed to be head boy," he said.

"I thought you were."

"I was going to refuse. But now I've made up my mind. I'll do it."

"Dorothy's head girl at the grammar school," she said.

Head boy, *head* girl, he thought. What a lot of nonsense it was. There were just boys and girls, people were just people.

"What about the plays?" he asked. "Shall we go together?"

"Yes," said Gloria. "I'd like to."

They agreed to see *Othello*, on the first of the two evenings; she would get the tickets, as they were on sale at the school. Andy wanted to pay for both, but she insisted that she should pay for her own.

It was a sort of date. It wasn't quite like going to the pictures, because that would have said very clearly that she was going out with him. A theatrical performance at which she paid for her own seat didn't mean that she was his girlfriend. But it was an improvement.

Perhaps there was a bit of glamour in being head boy.

The train journey in the morning was much the same. He couldn't say the behaviour was better or worse. Jackson had left, and there was no outstanding bully, but about half the compartments on the way to school were rough-houses. No one seemed to be seriously maltreated, but the boys came out of them looking dishevelled and red-faced; they were in an excitable mood, ready to run and to continue ragging about.

He couldn't care, really, whether they arrived at school all worked up and noisy, or not. But if he was supposed to be responsible for them, he thought that a less rowdy journey would make a lot of difference. He couldn't put a prefect in each compartment; there weren't enough of them, and they would never accept it anyway.

The solution would be to persuade the railway company to use the sort of carriages they had on the journey to Cornwall. These had no compartments, but were open all the way through. It would be in their own interest. When everyone could see what was happening, light bulbs wouldn't be smashed, mirrors cracked, upholstery torn.

But he couldn't approach the company himself. It would have to come from the head, and he hesitated about asking Old Man Harding. It would be interpreted as telling tales, or not being able to sort things out for yourself. The Old Man would never be prepared to admit that anything was wrong, that there was any bullying amongst the boys of Bywaters school.

However, he had said that he wanted a new style, and that meant more consultation. Andy decided to put his idea to him. After assembly at the village church, Harding was always the first to leave. He hared up the road to the school, ahead of the staff and pupils, and Andy chased after him.

The Old Man increased his pace as he heard someone coming up behind him. They were both almost running as Andy drew alongside, just before the drive to his private house.

"Could I have a word with you, sir?" he panted.

"What is it, *Trew*in?"

"About the railway, sir."

"Yes."

"I thought it would be better if there were open carriages."

99

"Open carriages?" he exclaimed. "Don't bother me now, *Trew*in."

"But, sir . . ."

Old Man Harding had entered the drive and hurried to the front door, leaving Andy on the path outside. He looked back towards the village; the teachers in their gowns were walking on the pavement, the first of the houses was marching up the centre of the road.

He felt annoyed. If the Old Man wouldn't listen to him, why should he try to do anything about it? The rough-houses could continue.

Andy hated wearing his navy-blue gaberdine raincoat; he preferred a scarf around his neck, and a cycling cape if it was wet. Although there was a school scarf in black and red, it was one of the Old Man's eccentricities that scarves and gloves should only be worn in extreme conditions. Some-times after church assembly he would inspect the houses, making the day-boys take off the offending garments. They were emblems of weakness; people who wore scarves were the first to go down with colds and flu.

Andy was determined not to wear his school raincoat when he was going out for the evening. There wasn't much opportunity to show a bit of style. He wore his school uniform, and tried to express himself by the way he threw his scarf nonchalantly around his neck. He had his big leather gauntlets for cycling.

Gloria wasn't ready and he had to wait for her.

"I didn't know what to wear," she explained when she came down. "I wanted to wear my new dress, but it would catch in the spokes."

She was wearing a tweed overcoat. It had a belt which she'd drawn in very tight at the waist. It made her look rather bundled up. She had put on lipstick for the occasion.

Again he felt how grown-up she looked. He liked the lipstick, he liked the feeling that he was taking her out. They rode to the grammar school.

In the hall they were shown to the second row of wooden chairs. He recognised a lot of people, Miss Baraclough and some of the teachers from sports day, and Dorothy Best, the new head girl. He wondered if Old Man Harding had ever seen a play; he was suddenly struck by how isolated the boys' school was.

In fact, Andy himself had never been to a play. There had never been any opportunity in Cornwall, and although there were theatres in Leeds and York, his parents never went out of Barnsby. He thought a theatrical performance was rather like going to church. He wouldn't try to hold Gloria's hand, or press close against her, especially as they were sitting right behind Miss Baraclough. They were not in a cinema. He would watch the play.

And once the play had begun, he couldn't think of anything else. He forgot all about Gloria, he forgot everything except what was happening on the stage. He had always enjoyed reading plays and imagining them in performance. He had acted in a sketch in the school concert last Easter; he knew that the idea of theatre excited him. But he had no idea that an actual stage production could be so overwhelming.

At the interval, when Miss Baraclough turned around and agreed with Gloria that it was very well done, that Othello was very good, he couldn't say anything. He felt completely removed from life in the school hall. Cyprus was more real than the dim civilities going on around him, and he waited for the interval to finish.

At the end of the play he clapped and clapped, trying to bring the actors and actresses back on stage once more, to prolong the magic. He couldn't bear it to end. It wasn't like reading; there was a satisfaction in reaching the last page and closing the book. He wanted the play to go on and on, like music. Finally, the curtain remained closed and the house lights went up. He shuffled out of the hall, aware of people pressing all around him, without really seeing any of them.

Outside, the evening air was cold; he breathed in deeply. Gloria was next to him. "What did you think of it?" she asked.

"Marvellous," he said. He felt dazed.

He didn't say much on the way home. He was still caught up in the feelings of the play.

It was getting dark as they turned into the lane. He had forgotten Gloria for most of the evening, but now that she was leaving he wanted to make the most of having gone out with her; it might not happen again. If they had been to the cinema, he could expect to kiss her goodnight. But they had been to a play, and there was no convenient tree-trunk by her gate, and his bicycle fettered him like a prisoner's ball and chain.

"Will you come tomorrow night?" he asked.

"Do you want to go *again*?" She seemed incredulous, as though it was excessive to want to see a play on two consecutive nights.

"Yes."

"Well, I don't," she said decisively.

"I shall go," he said.

The second time wasn't as good. The play was *The Misanthrope* by Molière, and it had been translated into rhyming couplets. Andy didn't feel the same involvement. When the interval came, instead of wanting to slump down in his chair, trying to hold on to what he had seen, he felt like stretching his legs. He got up and walked down the aisle. Then he saw that if he continued he would have to pass Dorothy, standing by the entrance, and he didn't particularly want to meet her. He stopped, and a man of about thirty, with sleek black hair, a dark suit and spotted bow tie, came up to him. It still seemed unusual to see anyone of his age out of uniform, and everyone else in the hall was either under twenty or over forty. He smiled as though he knew Andy.

"Hullo," he said.

"Hullo," said Andy.

"Are you enjoying it?"

"I preferred last night."

"I'm *so* glad," said the man. "I don't know how the French have the cheek to claim Molière as a second Shakespeare. There's *no* comparison." His voice was like an actor's. He accentuated certain words and spoke loudly, as though he expected everyone within hearing to listen, which they did.

"I thought last night was marvellous," said Andy.

"Yes," said the stranger. He spoke the word with a drawl, so that it sounded very uncertain. "It's a marvellous play, of course, but the production wasn't quite up to it, was it?" And he went on to tear it to pieces, bit by bit. The actor who played Othello didn't have the stature for the part. Iago never suggested the complexity of evil, but was merely a trouble-maker. Desdemona spoke prettily but showed no depth of character.

Andy began to feel very naïve. He hadn't watched the play critically at all; he had simply felt it. "It worked though," he said defensively.

"Of course it worked, because it's Shakespeare. The script is so good, it's almost impossible to ruin it – though they had a fairly good try." He described what he would have done, given the same company and the same conditions. He wouldn't have kept the painted backcloths for a start. He would have used a bare stage, as the Elizabethans did. He would have got rid of all the tatty old costumes, and performed the play in modern dress. The men would have had splendid uniforms instead of robes. He would have tried Bianca as Desdemona.

He was full of ideas, and they all seemed good ones. Andy now saw yesterday's production as very second-rate, and yet he resented the way his own experience of it had been diminished: he still stubbornly clung on to the feeling that there had been something good in it.

He reacted, too, against the self-assurance of the man in the bow tie. He was too superior, too sure that he was right. It was too much of a performance, done to draw the attention of everyone round about.

And yet Andy was impressed. The man certainly knew what he was talking about. Everyone else in the hall probably knew who he was; he must be a famous actor, writer or producer. Andy felt that he was the only one who had failed to recognise him.

"I don't think I know you," he said, meaning to sound apologetic.

"Oh, I know *you*," said the stranger. "In fact, I know a great deal about you."

It was very puzzling; no one as distinguished as this could know anything about Andy. The man was enjoying the effect he created, and he made it last.

"I've seen you on stage, for example," he went on. "I remember a *brilliant* demonstration of how to smoke a cigarette."

"Oh no," groaned Andy. He felt embarrassed; in the sketch last Easter he was supposed to smoke, but he couldn't light his cigarette so he kept his hand dangling at his side, hoping no one would notice.

"I was on the edge of my chair with suspense. The audience were on tenterhooks. Would he attempt to light it again or not?"

"It was dreadful," said Andy.

"It was *most* dramatic." He laughed very loud, so that people all over the hall turned to look. "What else do I know about you? I know that you're head boy at Bywaters, and the big white hope for a Cambridge scholarship."

"How do you know that?" Andy felt as though someone had been watching him for a long time, and he had known nothing about it.

The man in the bow tie stopped teasing, just at the moment when it would have become boring to continue any longer. His expression altered, and he said simply, "I'm a friend of Jim Carrington's."

It was strange to hear that Carrington had a first name, Jim, and that he even had a life outside the school.

"My name's Duncan Smith. I'm on the *Times and Echo*, you can read my review next week."

This was spoken in a rush, as the hall lights were going out two at a time. They went back to their seats.

Andy wondered if he would see him again, and was pleased to find that Duncan Smith appeared next to him in the slow procession out of the school at the end of the play. He wore a coat over his shoulders, without putting his arms into the sleeves. It made him look very sophisticated, like a real drama critic.

"I saw you here last night. You were with your" – he paused before choosing the word – "*enamorada*."

It was lost on Andy.

"Your girlfriend. Where is she tonight?"

"She didn't want to come."

"She reminded me of la Tosca."

"But she's not my girlfriend."

The audience for the play dispersed quickly, and soon they were the only two left at the gates of the school. The lights went out inside the building. There were a few street lights, widely spaced down the road; occasionally a car passed by.

Duncan talked and talked. He seemed to have seen every production in Stratford and London, to have read every book on the subject. He seemed to know personally a great many actors, some of them famous names.

The last cars disappeared from the streets, but Andy was incapable of making a move to go. Then the street lights went out, and Duncan became very apologetic for having kept him so long.

Andy rode off, standing on the pedals of his bike and forcing them round. The encounter left him with a feeling of excitement, as much as seeing the play had the night before. He felt elated all the way home, and couldn't go to sleep for a long time.

There could be no doubt about it; things were getting worse on the train in the morning. Andy couldn't pretend otherwise. He walked the length of the platform, feeling like a gauleiter in the SS. As long as he patrolled up and down, it was all very orderly. There was no running about, no changing from compartment to compartment; everyone was quiet. A visitor travelling on the train for the first time would be very impressed.

But Andy sensed a suppressed excitement in the air, a feeling that everyone was waiting. He stood by the door of the prefects' compartment. Pugsley arrived; he was grinning as though he too was biding his time. The guard blew his whistle and waved his green flag.

Andy got in and sat down. The train began to move, and almost immediately the noise started. It could be heard above the steam from the engine and the grinding of the wheels. It sounded as though there was a rough-house in every compartment.

"You've got to do something about it," said Reg, looking up from his *Daily Mirror*.

"Yes, but what?" asked Andy. Short of walking along the running board, there was no way he could influence what was happening in each of the compartments, once the train was under way. The only thing he could do was lean out of the window.

There were boys hanging out all the way along the train, some as far as the waist. They were shouting and waving.

"Get your heads in," he bawled. "Featherstone, come to the study at break."

The old incantation seemed to work, though rather slowly. Eventually all heads were inside, and the train continued noisily down the track.

Featherstone reported to the study. He was a small, cheerful sort of boy. "You were behaving like a maniac," said Andy. "What did you do it for?"

"It's fun."

There was a style for telling people off, in which you picked up what they had said and turned it against them. Duckworth was expert at it; his next line would have been, "Perhaps you'll find *this* fun." But Andy rejected it.

"You can lose your break."

"Oh, no, *Trew*in."

"And you'll lose it every day if you go on being a nuisance on the train."

"I've got to see a friend."

"Go into room one."

"I'd rather be beaten, it gets it over quickly." He bent over, pulling up the bottom of his jacket. His elbows stuck out, and he hopped around the floor, presenting his backside. "Beat me, please. Beat me." He looked and sounded like a young bird.

Everyone laughed. Andy pushed him out and saw him into room one, opposite.

"Is it true," asked Gloria, "that you won't beat anybody?"

She had finished her piano practice, and they were walking down to the canal. It was colder now, and she wore slacks and a thick brown sweater with a floppy roll-over collar. He had his scarf around his neck.

"Yes."

"Why not?"

"I don't believe in it."

He knew what she would think; that it was one more tradition gone. Bywaters was going to rack and ruin.

"I don't admire you for it," she said.

"I don't care."

"I like someone who's strong and powerful, a leader."

Andy clicked his heels together and gave a Nazi salute. "*Heil Hitler*," he said.

"No," she said, "but someone I can respect. It won't make you popular, you know."

"I know *that*." He had no illusion that he was some sort of liberator, freeing the populace from the bondage under which they had suffered. There would be no cheering.

"Our Bobby says the train's like a madhouse these days."

"It'll settle down," said Andy, though he had no confidence that it would. He would have liked to talk about it, but Gloria would only say what the prefects said at school.

He changed the subject. He wanted to talk about *Othello*, if only to remind her that she had gone with him. He said he thought that the actor who played Othello didn't have the stature for the part, that Iago didn't convey the depth of evil.

"You've changed your tune," said Gloria.

"I've had time to think about it."

"You sound just like Dorothy. She said the same things."

He felt ashamed. Dorothy must have thought them out for herself. He was very good at taking other people's opinions and passing them off as his own; that was all his essay-writing amounted to.

"I wish they came to Barnsby more often," he said.

"There's always the pictures."

He leaped at the opportunity, not knowing – and not caring – whether she had said it deliberately, or whether it was just chance. "Will you come with me on Friday?"

She agreed to go out with him.

"*Trew*in, could you do me a favour?" asked Carrington at the end of the lesson in the library.

"Yes, sir."

"Come up to my room and I'll explain."

Reg cleared his throat twice, and then tried to disguise it by going into a fit of coughing. Andy wondered what Carrington wanted as he followed him.

He sat down in one of the easy chairs, and Carrington made coffee. There was something different about his attitude, as though he was uncertain about what he was going to ask.

"I've had a phone call from our mutual friend," he began. Andy thought he was talking about the Dickens' novel, and couldn't make sense of it. "I gather you've met Duncan Smith?"

"Oh yes," said Andy.

"He lent me some books, which he wants back rather hurriedly. He wondered if you could drop them in on your way home this evening."

He was delighted to do it.

"I've parcelled them up. They're . . . ah . . . on the table." He pointed to the large brown envelope. He hesitated; he seemed to be reluctant about something. "Look, Duncan's all right," he said. "But I want to . . . ah . . . warn you about him."

Andy looked surprised.

"He talks too much. Don't let him . . . ah . . . distract you. Keep you from your work, you know."

"Oh no," said Andy.

The address was in Church Walk, a terrace of houses separated from the churchyard by a path which led to the vicarage. The railings were intact, and a notice said that cycling was prohibited. Andy pushed his bike to number five. There were big yellow leaves from the plane trees on the ground. He propped his bike against a low wall.

He went up the steps to the front door. The envelope was too big to go through the letterbox. He pulled the bell knob, and heard the bell ringing inside the house. A buxom, grey-haired woman came to the door. Andy was explaining that he was leaving some books for Mr Smith, when Duncan came leaping down the stairs.

"Andrew, come on up. It's *so* good of you to bring the books. Tell me, how's Jimmy?"

Jimmy? thought Andy, and then remembered it was Carrington. How was he? You never thought how teachers were.

He was surprised that Duncan was at home; he had

expected him to be at work. He went up the stairs to a room on the first floor at the front of the house. Through the window were the half-bare branches of a tree, and beyond that the graveyard and the church.

The landlady came in with a tray covered with a lace cloth and laden with very dainty china, tea and scones.

"Bless you, Mrs Saxon, you're an absolute angel," said Duncan. "Where should I be without you?"

The lady blushed and retired.

"Oh dear," sighed Duncan. "I think she's fallen in love with me. I don't know *what* I do to cause it."

Having heard the way he spoke to her, Andy had a pretty good idea, but he didn't say anything.

"She lost her husband in the war, I'm sure she thinks I'm going to marry her. I shall have to move into a flat again."

Andy wished war widows would fall in love with him.

"I lived in a flat when I first came here, but after a while it became so squalid. I hate getting meals and washing up, I was driven into lodgings. Now I get everything done for me, but I have to eat with Mrs Saxon and make polite conversation." He leaned forward towards Andy. "Do you think I ought to marry her?"

"No," said Andy, surprised.

"Why not?"

"Well . . . you don't want to." The whole idea was preposterous. Andy couldn't understand why he pretended to consider it.

He went on to weigh up all the advantages and disadvantages of being married, being looked after in lodgings, and living in a flat. It all seemed rather unrealistic to Andy.

The church clock struck five. Duncan jumped up. "I promised James I wouldn't keep you a minute after the hour," he said. "I don't think he quite trusts me, I can't imagine why. I swore to him on the phone, I'd be on my *best* behaviour."

They went down to the front door. "By the way," said Duncan. "Next Friday I'm going to a student production of

Doctor Faustus at Leeds University. Would you like to come?"

Andy jumped at the chance. Then he remembered. "I've promised to go out," he said.

"Ah, la Tosca," said Duncan.

"Yes." He wanted to go to the pictures with Gloria, and he also wanted to see the play at Leeds with Duncan. For years he never went anywhere, and suddenly two opportunities occurred on the same day. He couldn't decide.

"Well, we can't let la Tosca down, can we?" said Duncan. "I could change to Saturday evening if you like."

Andy's heart leaped up. He could have both the things he wanted.

They padlocked their bicycles together and left them against the cinema wall. Andy paid, while Gloria was still struggling with her purse trying to find the money. The usherette showed them to a double seat at the back.

As soon as they sat down, Gloria tried to make him take the ticket money, but he refused. She didn't give up, and they went on passing it from one to the other until a shilling dropped on the floor, and then he had to scrabble around under the seats to pick it up.

He plonked the coin in her lap, and the lights went down. This was the moment he had been waiting for; he knew he had to put his arm around her straight away, otherwise the longer he left it the more difficult it would be. The advertisements appeared on the screen, slides for local businesses: Mumby's Taxis, Skiptons for bread and high-class confectionery, Butterfield the butcher . . . Gloria gave him a nudge, and he slid his arm around her shoulders. She snuggled up against him.

The slides finished, and the filmed advertisements were shown. Some of them were very funny: they were made for distribution all over the country, and left a gap at the end for the name of the local firm. A magnificent Parisian fashion display was followed by Pogson and Sons, Drapers and

Outfitters, High Street; the discrepancy appealed to Andy. Then came *For Your Future Entertainment*, the trailers for the films to come. The lights went up, and he rather guiltily withdrew his arm.

He glanced around. Some of the couples had moved apart, others were still necking, oblivious of the interval, their faces pressed together and their arms entwined. The usherettes were coming up the gangway with their lit-up trays of ice-cream.

"Would you like an ice-cream?" he asked.

She shook her head. He was glad, because he couldn't really afford it, but worse still, he imagined her holding on to it and making it last halfway through the film, digging into the tub and licking the little wooden spoon.

"Do you want one?" she asked.

"No," he said, very definitely.

As soon as the lights went down, he put his arm around her again and tried to smooch, but she turned her head away. He tried to follow, but then his head was in her way, and she indicated by an impatient push of her shoulders that she wanted to watch the film.

It was a costume drama, with James Mason and Margaret Lockwood, and Andy wasn't very interested in it. He kept telling himself that he was in a double seat in the cinema, with his arm around Gloria – and it wasn't as good as it should have been. She was wearing her heavy tweed coat; it was more like embracing a great bulky parcel than a person. She must be boiling hot.

With his left hand he felt for her belt and gradually began to slide the heavy material through the clasp. It wasn't easy doing it with one hand, and so stealthily that she didn't seem to know what he was doing. It took him quite a while, and when it was done he started on the buttons, one after another until he could turn back the two folds of the coat. She leaned against him, totally absorbed in the film.

What next? he wondered. The fingers of his free hand crept back to her middle, and he felt for the buttons on her dress. There didn't seem to be any, so they crept higher and higher, until she suddenly seemed to notice what he was doing. She took his hand in hers and held it on her lap, more to imprison it than as a gesture of affection.

He withdrew after a while and looked for fresh fields. With his full attention on the screen, he dropped his hand on her knee, and she didn't try to hold it in her lap again. He reached lower and slid his hand under her skirt, returning to her knee but this time beneath the material. Very slowly, at the pace at which continents move across the surface of the world, his fingers moved up her nylon stockings.

After a long time, he felt a change of terrain. He had reached the top. His fingers started to march up her suspender.

Wham! The slap on his wrist came at a very tense and silent moment in the film, and resounded through the cinema. It was probably harder than Gloria intended. People nearby sniggered. A man called out, "Watch it, lad! Don't go too far," and those who heard laughed and then other people in the front turned round and shushed, telling them to be quiet, that they wanted to watch the film.

In a moment it had all subsided. Andy withdrew his arm from Gloria's shoulder – it was quite dead, anyway – and slumped down in his seat. He put his hands on his lap, and felt grateful for the darkness.

She brushed down her skirt, and reached across and took his hand.

They rode home in the dark. He was thinking about the goodnight kiss. It was no good leaving it until they were at her gate. It was too public, there was the light from her house and the other houses.

As they reached the oak tree opposite the lane, he swung off the road.

"What are you doing?" she asked, but she followed him. The light of their bicycle lamps showed up every indentation in the bark of the oak. "I want to say goodnight," he said.

"We can say goodnight outside my house."

"It's not the same," said Andy.

They switched off their lights to save the batteries, and propped the bikes against the tree. It was completely dark. Andy felt for Gloria; she was leaning against the trunk. Her elbows were against the trunk, too, and she used her forearms as props to keep him at a certain distance. "I don't want to kiss you," she said.

"Why not?"

"Kissing is serious. I don't want to kiss on the lips. I don't mind anywhere else."

He could see nothing of her face. He found her eyes and kissed them, the edge of her hair, her neck.

"Just once," he pleaded.

She kissed him quickly on the mouth.

He tried to reach between the buttons of her coat. "No," she said fimly, pushing him away. "I've got to be going."

She found her bike and switched on the lamp. The light spread upwards, picking out the golden leaves of the oak tree.

Duncan drove a pre-war Standard Ten, dark green in colour. He parked in the road outside their house, and Andy introduced him to his parents. They called him Mr Smith at first, but were soon calling him Duncan. Apart from that, it was like a visit from one of the teachers; they talked about Andy, his progress at school and his plans for the future. Duncan must have heard a lot from Carrington, because he knew all Andy's strengths and weaknesses – he was very perceptive, but not so good at constructing an argument, he wrote well but was sometimes rather shallow. It was like a school report, and his parents listened deferentially, until Duncan's friendliness made them feel at ease.

Andy had wondered how Duncan would behave with his parents; they wouldn't have liked the way he showed off at the play, but he was quite different here. Charming, sensible, very keen that their son should get to Cambridge: it was difficult to remember that he wasn't a teacher.

He had taken a degree in English at London University and was then called-up into the army. He had finished the war as a major, a fact which impressed Mr Trewin. In the talk about education, Andy learned that his mother hadn't gone on to higher education because it would have meant leaving Cornwall, and her family expected her to stay at home. He hadn't known that before.

Then his dad launched into the story of how he came to be in Yorkshire, and how they wouldn't dare treat him like that if he'd had more education. Duncan listened sympathetically.

As soon as they were in the car, Duncan turned to him and said, "Gosh, they're nice people."

"Oh," said Andy, surprised. He had never thought of them as nice or not, they were just his parents.

"They're very proud of you, you know."

"Oh," said Andy again. He wasn't used to discussing family feelings and relationships.

"They expect a lot of you."

"That's the trouble, everyone does," said Andy.

They drove on towards Leeds. Duncan talked about his own family. His father had died from injuries received during the First World War, and he had been brought up by his mother. From the way he talked about her, Andy couldn't make out whether he was very attached to her, or whether he couldn't stand her. He didn't see her very often.

"What will you do after Cambridge?" Duncan asked.

"If I get in," said Andy. He didn't know. He hadn't thought yet beyond getting there, though he had recently felt that he would like to do something connected with plays. He knew he hadn't seen much theatre, and he was no good as an actor – he couldn't even light a cigarette – but later perhaps, when he had more experience, there might be something he could do. Really, he'd like to belong to a company of travelling players, like the Open Door.

Duncan talked about his own plans. He had come back to civilian life without a job. He had started a higher degree but abandoned it for a training scheme to become a journalist. After a few months on the *Times and Echo* he hoped to move to a national paper. "Fleet Street, here I come," he announced.

But he was surprisingly uncertain about it. He was afraid that he might remain a local reporter for ever. Andy couldn't understand it. He thought that someone like Duncan Smith would be able to do whatever he wanted. He had taken a degree, he had become a major in the army; he could easily become a drama critic on a London paper. If *he* couldn't do it, nobody could.

"I'm getting old," he said. "I shall be thirty next birthday. And anyone who's going to do anything will have done it by the time he's thirty."

"You can't count the war years," said Andy.

"Oh yes you can," said Duncan. "There are plenty of people who made use of them to further their careers. I've done nothing yet."

"There's still time."

"But it's running out. I think I'm going to be one of those people who are eternally promising, always expected to do something remarkable and yet never quite getting round to it. I shall probably go to my grave still full of promise, but with the great masterpiece unwritten."

It seemed terribly sad. Suddenly Duncan began singing *Don't put your daughter on the stage, Mrs Worthington*, tapping the steering wheel as an accompaniment, and the mood changed. He knew all the words, and did a good imitation of Noel Coward, though Andy was a bit alarmed about his driving.

"*You* ought to be on the stage," he said, when he had finished. Duncan laughed.

Andy was wary of making any comments on *Doctor Faustus*; he knew he enjoyed plays too much to be critical of them. He could see, though, that the comic scenes weren't very successful, and that some of the undergraduates taking part were rather self-conscious. He waited to hear what Duncan had to say; secretly he thought it was excellent.

Duncan had his say at the interval, when they went backstage and discussed the production with the producer, a university lecturer whom Duncan knew already. He became even more theatrical than ever. Andy felt embarrassed for him, but it didn't seem to bother anyone else. In fact, they all behaved in the same sort of way. Andy kept quiet, and absorbed his first impression of university life.

They talked about the play on the way home. In some ways it was like a lesson, except that Duncan could talk about books and plays as though they mattered, without making a lecture of it. He was better at this than Carrington.

They arrived opposite the house. There was a light in the hall, but no other light in any of the houses in the row. Duncan switched off the engine.

"What you said earlier, about everyone expecting a lot from you," he said, lighting a cigarette, "does it worry you?"

"Being head boy does."

"In what way?"

Andy told him all about the train in the morning. "The solution's easy," he said, "if only they'd put on different carriages, without compartments."

"Can't you get Harding to do anything about it?"

"He won't listen."

"Are you sure?"

"I've tried twice now."

Duncan was silent for a while.

"You've got to force his hand," he said. "Couldn't you make use of the *Times and Echo* in some way? If I wrote an article about the train journey, would that help? It might make him take notice."

"It would make him furious."

"And he'd probably blame you." Duncan thought again, drawing on his cigarette and exhaling the smoke. "I could ring him up to say that I was *thinking* of writing an article about the journey to school. You know, part of the local scene, a tradition that's been going on for years. I could ask him when it started, has the train ever failed to get through, and so on. Then I could hint at rumours of vandalism and say I was going to travel on the train myself."

"That might work," said Andy. "He can't stand publicity."

"And we could keep the article in reserve, just in case he doesn't do anything about it." Duncan seemed delighted with the scheme.

Andy stored up everything that happened, as though he was making a running commentary for Duncan, or writing him a continuous letter. He was thinking about him in the third lesson on Monday morning, at the time when he knew Duncan planned to phone the school. In his mind he could hear Duncan's voice on the phone, smooth and charming. He knew exactly what he would say, and what the Old Man would reply.

It wasn't long before the secretary, Beverley or Valerie, came tit-tupping down the length of the library in her high heels. She blushed as she gave her message: "The headmaster would like to see *Trew*in straight away in his study."

Andy followed her, his eyes on her skirt. He stepped ahead to open a door. She looked at him, and he gave her a wink.

"Ah, *Trew*in," said Old Man Harding, looking up from his desk. "What's the behaviour like on the train these days?"

Duncan's phone call was having its effect.

"It's bad, sir," said Andy. He had had time to prepare his

answer. If the question had been sprung on him, he would probably have said, in Bywaters fashion, that everything was all right.

Harding looked startled. "What's going on, lad?"

"There's a lot of rough-housing."

"Is it worse than it used to be?"

"It's always been bad," said Andy.

The head sucked on his pipe. "What impression would a member of the public have?"

"There wouldn't be a rough-house in his compartment, but he'd hear it going on all around him."

"What happens in a rough-house?"

"There are different sorts," said Andy. "Some are just free-for-alls, some pick on the first and second years, some attack the carriage."

"What do they do?"

"Smash the bulbs, swing from the racks, tear the upholstery. That sort of thing."

"Good God," exclaimed Harding. "Did this happen in Duckworth's time?"

"It's always happened," said Andy. Then honesty compelled him to add, "It's particularly bad at the moment."

"We've got to clamp down on it," said the Old Man. "Pick out two or three trouble-makers and I'll deal with them in assembly tomorrow."

"I can't," said Andy.

"Why not?"

"Because it happens in closed compartments. That's the trouble, you can't see what's going on. There's not even a corridor."

"Pick them up as they come out."

"I don't know who they are."

"You must do."

"Last year Jackson was the worst, but this year it's much more general."

"Jackson? I thought he was a splendid fellow."

"The best solution would be to get the railways to put on open carriages. I don't think there would be any problem then."

He had to explain what he meant by open carriages, as Harding seemed to have a picture of coal trucks open to the sky. In his heart he probably believed that this was the most suitable form of transport for boys. Andy explained that they were used on long-distance trains; you could walk down the centre and there were groups of seats on either side. "The advantage is, you can see everybody all the time."

Old Man Harding got up and walked over to the window. Andy knew what he was thinking; how could you ask the railway to change the system, without admitting that something was wrong?

He stared out into his autumn garden for a while. There were big clumps of Michaelmas daisies outside the window. Then he turned and said, "Thank you, *Trew*in. That's all."

"But what about the carriages?"

"I'll give it some thought, lad."

Andy called at Church Walk on his way home. Duncan was still enjoying their plot; there was something schoolboyish about his enthusiasm.

"Old Man Harding was *very* suspicious," he said. He re-enacted what he had said on the phone, and Harding's replies. He caricatured both himself and the Old Man; it was very believable. "Finally Harding said he was busy and would ring back later. That's when he must have sent for you."

Andy described his interview, just as it had happened.

"Then later in the day he rang back," Duncan continued. "'Now listen here, Smith,' he said. 'We're having a new look at travel arrangements. It's all in melting pot at moment. I'd greatly appreciate it if you could hold on for time being.'

"'What changes are you considering, Mr Harding?'

"'I've been in touch with railway company, and they're contemplating putting new carriages on line. So if you could wait until these come into operation, I'd be much obliged.'

"'Of course, Mr Harding. We're always delighted to help the school in any way we can.' And with many salaams and greetings, I rang off."

Andy laughed. "Poor Old Harding," he said. "It's been a busy day for him."

Just before half-term, he had another call to the study. He walked alongside the secretary, her footsteps on the tiled floor echoing down the corridor.

"Do they call you Beverley?" he asked.

"Valerie."

"Do you like working here?"

"It's very interesting," she said.

She lived in the village; it was a pity she didn't travel from Barnsby.

"Ah, *Trew*in," said the head. "I just wanted to tell you that after half-term, there'll be open-plan carriages on the train. It's all arranged."

"Very good, sir."

"Let me know if there's any trouble."

At break Andy told the prefects. There was some moaning from those who didn't like any sort of change – they'd lose their privacy, the prefects had always had their own compartment and now they'd have to travel with everyone else. But most of them recognised the improvement, and agreed to do what they could to make the first day go smoothly.

He told Gloria when they went to the pictures the following Friday, after they had broken up for a long weekend. They had both more or less assumed that once they had gone out together, they would continue going to the pictures as a weekly date.

"That's one more tradition gone," she said, as she unbelted her coat all down the middle.

"A good job too," said Andy, putting his arm around her shoulder, even before the lights went down.

"They've always had rough-houses. When our dad was at Bywaters, it used to be *murder*."

"There you are," said Andy.

"It didn't do them any harm."

"How do you know?"

"It didn't harm our dad." She snuggled up against him. "I think it's a shame, all the old traditions going."

They settled down to enjoy the programme. What she liked was to watch a film, preferably romantic, and cuddle close to him. She had set the limits; he knew how far he could go, and knowing he would get no further, he might as well watch the film – after all, he had paid to see it. Occasionally, when the story bored him, he would try to explore, but there was not much conviction in it and he was easily repulsed.

"Who's this Duncan?" she asked in the interval. Andy had briefly mentioned his part in getting the head to do something about the train.

"He's a friend of Carrington's," said Andy. It seemed presumptuous to say he was a friend of his.

"Is he a teacher?"

"No, he's on the *Times and Echo*. But he's more like a teacher."

"Oh," said Gloria.

It was a beautiful day in late October, as warm as summer. The countryside looked perfect; the stubble fields were newly ploughed, and the woods were golden brown. They drove along with the sunroof drawn back, and the windows wide open. The wind blew against their open-necked shirts.

Duncan turned off the road, and bumped across a meadow down to the river bank. There were a few willows with long yellow leaves, and a broad sweep of water to the opposite bank. There was no one around.

"It's a good place for swimming," he said. "I came here a lot in the summer. It was always crowded then."

They sat and watched the water between the low banks. "Come on, let's go in."

"I haven't got a costume."

"That doesn't matter. There's no one here."

"I'm not going in without."

"My dear, we are prudish, aren't we?" Duncan said. He started to strip off by the side of the car. "You'll find my trunks on the back seat if you want to borrow them."

Andy changed and followed Duncan to the water's edge. The bank had crumbled away and there was a sandy beach amongst the willows, with a spit of sand stretching out into the water. The river swept around it in a curve beyond.

Duncan waded through the shallow water, and dived with a splash. His back gleamed wet on the surface. He turned and waved.

Andy ran into the water. It was freezing cold. He dived, and the shock of the cold took his breath away. He stood up, spluttering and shaking the water off himself, and then dived again. He began to swim vigorously.

"Don't go out too far," shouted Duncan. "There's a current."

Already they had been swept several yards downriver, and they began to force their way against the stream. They became warm with the effort. Once they were some distance beyond the beach, they stopped struggling and let the current take them back. They drifted into shallow water.

Andy left first. As soon as he was out of the water, he felt cold and began to shiver. "Have you got a towel?" he called. *Fetch tow-el*, he could hear the voice of the girl at the swimming baths.

Duncan threw him one from the back of the car. He didn't seem to feel the cold; he tied a rug around his middle, wearing it like a long skirt, and lit a cigarette. He came and took the towel from Andy and rubbed his back, and then his hair. His cigarette dangled from his lips, and he rubbed in a professional sort of way, like a boxing trainer.

They sat in the sun to finish drying off. Duncan had ended the war in Italy. He loved the Italians; he found them so spontaneous, so friendly, so *simpatico*. He thought the people in Yorkshire were very dour. "They're so proud of what they call their frankness," he said. "I'd call it just bloody rudeness."

Andy found himself defending Yorkshire.

"We could go to Italy next summer," said Duncan. "You will have finished your exams, and I shall have finished at the *Times and Echo*. We could get in the car and drive down to Naples. Why not?"

Andy couldn't believe he meant it. He wanted very much to go abroad. When Oldershaw had come back from France after the summer holidays, he had kept staring at him, as though some difference ought to show, although he seemed exactly the same and Andy felt disappointed. But to go to Italy . . .

He refused to allow himself even to think it was possible, and Duncan went on planning, saying that they would need very little money, he had so many friends who would put them up and the people were so generous. He talked about Italians he knew and their families; he smoked several cigarettes before they changed.

They drove on to York. Andy hadn't seen the city before, and they walked on the Roman walls and through the Shambles and into the Minster. They went to a cafe which Duncan had found on an earlier visit. He was eager to show it to Andy.

"Voilà," he said, as he made his entrance, gesturing around the room as though he owned it. "C'est magnifique, n'est-ce pas?"

It was all green and gold; there were gilt chairs and glass-topped tables, and the waitresses wore green and cream uniforms. A trio surrounded by potted plants and palms played semi-classical music; a man in evening dress sat at the piano and two women in long dresses played a violin and a cello.

They went up thickly carpeted stairs to a gallery, from where they could look down on the trio and the tables below. The cafe was crowded with Saturday afternoon shoppers, many of them women in fur coats despite the warm weather.

They sat at a table with a lamp on it. The lighting was dim, and people were talking in hushed voices.

"Qu'est-ce que vous prennez?" asked Duncan loudly.

And to Andy's dismay, he continued to speak only in French. He pretended that Andy could speak no English, and he explained everything to him, how the English love their tea, and how typically English the cafe was. "C'est très amusant."

All the customers had stopped talking and turned round to look at them. Suppose some of them really were French, thought Andy. Duncan translated the menu: "Oeufs sur toast, fromage sur toast, haricots sur toast."

The waitress came over to their table.

"Bonjour, mademoiselle," exclaimed Duncan. "Avez-vous . . . 'ave you . . . thé de Chine?"

"Sheen?" asked the waitress.

"Oui, tea of Chine."

The girl was puzzled.

"La Chine," said Duncan, and he put his forefingers to his eyes and drew them back to make them look oriental.

"Japanese," said the girl.

"Non, non, non. La Chine. Comment appelle-t-on ça en anglais?" He appealed to Andy.

"Sheen-a," said Andy.

"China," said the waitress. "China tea."

"Ah, oui!" Duncan and the waitress celebrated their success. Andy felt sorry for her; she was very busy.

When she served them, Duncan said *merci* and *très bien* and *merveilleux* a great many times, and the waitress seemed very flattered. She gave them all her attention and neglected the other customers.

Duncan didn't have much more French than a schoolboy, but he made a little go a long way. "Et maintenant, mon cher," he said. "Qui sera la mère?"

"Vous," said Andy.

Duncan poured the *Lapsang Souchong*. He waited for Andy to taste it. "Comment le trouvez-vous?" he asked.

Andy thought it was strange to drink tea with lemon instead of milk. He wanted to like it, but he really preferred the Typhoo tea they drank at home.

"Très bien," he said doubtfully.

Duncan laughed, and his laughter filled the café, drowning the tinkling of the piano and the scraping of bowstrings.

After tea, they went to the repertory company at the Theatre Royal. The set represented a country house, with oak panelling, latticed windows and chintz-covered furniture. The play was a comedy, of the *anyone-for-tennis* type; the production was slick and professional.

They drove back in the dark, and stopped again in the road outside the Trewins' house.

"This had better be the last of our outings for a while," Duncan said.

Andy was disappointed.

"You've less than half a term left. You ought to be working flat out."

"Is that Carrington's idea?"

"No, it's my own. But I'll see you around. Let me know if there's any way I can help. All right?"

"I suppose so."

"Ciao," said Duncan. He dropped his hand on to Andy's knee, and gave it a squeeze.

On Tuesday morning, the first morning back at school after

the long weekend for half-term, the engine backed two carriages into Barnsby station.

The boys on the platform saw that they were different, and fell silent. They watched with curiosity, and then there was a sudden burst of comment. The doors were at either end of each carriage. They entered suspiciously, looking up and down, surprised to find themselves in one long carriage instead of a small compartment. The bench seats faced each other, in groups of four on one side and six on the other. They sat down, keeping places for friends.

And although Andy and the prefects were ready to stop them moving about, there was no need. The prefects took over the ten seats at the end, on either side of the centre passage, and none of them felt very deprived. After one tour through the two carriages, Andy and Pugsley sat down with the others. Everything was quiet.

It looked as though rough-houses would be a thing of the past. Andy could even have a twinge of regret for them.

His mum and dad went to a chapel concert on Friday evening. It was most unusual for them to go out, and he wanted to make the most of the opportunity.

"Will you come to our house?" he asked Gloria.

"What for?"

"There's nothing much on at the pictures."

"All right," she agreed.

He was glad it was dark, so that none of the neighbours could see them going in together. He showed her into the living room. He had banked up a huge coal fire and pulled the settee across the front of it. He felt embarrassed, because as he came back into the room it all looked so obviously set up. He saw Gloria taking it all in.

"Shall I take your coat?" he asked, hovering around her.

She took it off; she was wearing a skirt and blouse. The blouse was like a shirt, with buttons all the way to the waist, and there were more buttons down to the hem of the skirt. He hung up her overcoat on the hall stand.

127

She sat on the edge of the settee and held her hands to the fire, as though she was cold. The settee was covered with brown rexine; it was hard and shiny, and never got warm. He picked up the cushions from the other chair and dropped them behind her.

"Would you like some coffee?" he asked.

"Shall I help?"

"No, I can do it." He went into the kitchen and made two mugs of coffee; he placed them on the tiles of the fire surround. He switched on the radio, tuning in to the music on the Light Programme; he turned the volume low. He would have liked to turn the lights down low, too, but there was only one, an electric bulb under a glass shade in the centre of the room.

They drank their coffee, and then he sat next to her. It was like a double seat in the cinema, with the flames of the coal fire to look at instead of a screen. He put his arm around her.

It was like the cinema in some ways, but it was also unlike it. It was more tense. There were no people around; they were alone in the house and anything could happen. The only sound was the background music and occasionally a coal dropping in the grate.

With his left hand he felt around her waist. He undid a button and slipped inside her blouse. He touched bare flesh; she wasn't wearing a slip or vest. His hand slid up under her arm; he felt a slight bulge, and then the tight band of elastic. Very slowly he moved along the elastic towards the front; he felt the material change, and then the swelling of her breast. He hardly dared to move, in case she noticed. She stirred, and he froze.

She took his hand, and held it in her lap. He felt unable to speak, even to think. "Why not?" he managed to say.

"Why should I?"

He had no answer. He tried to put his hand back and she pushed him away.

He pleaded with her. "Why won't you let me?"

"Because it means too much to you."

He was completely taken aback. "You mean, if I didn't care about it, you would?"

"Maybe."

He groaned. He couldn't express what he wanted to say. It seemed so unfair, he thought she was refusing for the very reason that she ought to say yes, because he had strong feelings about her.

"You're too intense," she said.

He moved away from her to the other end of the settee, and stared into the fire. He felt that he was almost choking, he couldn't say a word.

Everything was quiet. "Put the light out then," she said.

He couldn't believe it at first. He turned and looked at her. Her face was solemn.

He got up awkwardly, and stumbled to the switch. In the sudden blackness he bumped against the furniture as he groped his way back to the end of the settee. Then the light from the fire made the room bright but mysterious, with shadows on the wall. It glowed on Gloria's dark hair and her face looked ruddy. It was like the lighting in a picture.

Frowning slightly, she undid the rest of the buttons on her blouse. She drew apart the two sides like curtains, to reveal her brassière. She tossed back her hair, and sat rather stiff and upright, staring down at the two white ramparts.

Andy gazed at them too. He made a movement forward, and she immediately snatched the sides of her blouse together. "Ah," she said warningly.

He knelt before her, casting a huge shadow over the room. She sat in a more relaxed way, leaning forward slightly, letting her blouse hang loose, her arms on the cushions. He placed his hands on her waist, then passed them over her bra. He reached behind her back and fumbled with the fastener.

"Oh, you're pinching me," she said.

"You undo it."

"No."

Her manner changed. She was like a nanny who had been indulgent with the children, but now there would be no more spoiling. She sat up in a way which said very clearly that the party was over.

When she had gone, he looked up a poem in a book he had been given as a school prize, an anthology collected by a war-time general. The poem was Andrew Marvell's "To his coy mistress". He thought how appropriate it was, more so than he remembered; they even shared the same name.

On Sunday afternoon he took the book, with its gilt school crest on the cover, to the Butterfields'. Gloria was in the front room doing her homework. He read it to her, particularly relishing some of the couplets.

"*Had we but world enough, and time, This coyness, lady, were no crime . . . My vegetable love should grow vaster than empires, and more slow . . . Two hundred years to adore each breast, But thirty thousand to the rest.*"

He changed his voice dramatically. "*But at my back I always hear Time's wingèd chariot hurrying near; And yonder all before us lie Deserts of vast eternity.*" He glanced up to see how she would react to the next bit: "*then worms shall try That long preserved virginity, And your quaint honour turn to dust, And into Ashes all my lust.*"

It seemed to carry more weight than he intended. He was being too intense again. He tried to finish more nonchalently with the appeal to "*sport us while we may . . . And tear our pleasures with rough strife Thorough the iron gates of life.*"

Gloria was romantic, and she was either moved by the poem, or the idea of his reading it. When he closed the book and turned to her, she gave him, there in her own front room, his first full-length, feature-film kiss. And lips were serious, she had said.

He had never really liked Gloria all that much. But now he felt quite emotional; he felt fond of her, in a *Good-Old-Gloria* sort of way. He would have done anything for her.

Guy Fawkes Night was still a special celebration, because there hadn't been any fireworks and bonfires during the war. The people in Gloria's lane had built an enormous pile of wood on a piece of waste ground between the houses, and Andy joined her just before it was set alight.

It was a cold evening, with a wind from the north-east. There were groups of people standing about; Andy and Gloria bumped into them in the dark. Voices came out of the blackness, and children were running about. There were torches of different brightness all over the place.

A man lit the bonfire. A shower of sparks shot up into the wind. The dry wood caught quickly, and soon the flames were leaping into the air, lighting up people's faces and sending distorted shadows across the ground.

There were a few fireworks: some bangers which made people jump and Roman candles which made them all breathe out a communal sigh as the firework sparkled and flamed. "Ah, in't it luvly," said several voices. The Catherine wheels were a bit of a disappointment, failing to go round, or shooting off from their posts. Rockets whizzed into the sky.

Gloria didn't like the jumping crackers. They were the favourites of her brother Bob and his friends. She would hear them hissing and see the fuse burning, and then they would start exploding and jumping, and she would leap around Andy, holding on to him.

The boys laughed, including Andy, and Bob threw one right at her feet. She was so mad she got hold of him and boxed his ears, really hard. Andy had never seen anything like it.

Mrs Butterfield had cooked faggots and peas for everyone, and she served them from a table; there were candles in jars, two big metal pans, and piles of plates and forks. Mr Butterfield, who had made the faggots, stood grinning by her side.

Everyone was being very jolly, making jokes about eating the peas with a fork. There was a strong sense of togetherness, as there had been in the war. Andy wished his mum and dad had come; the Butterfields had invited them, but they had stayed at home. Perhaps they would have felt out of it.

They took their plates of faggots and peas, and sat down on a bank not far from the blaze. Their backs were cold in the north-east wind, their fronts roasted by the fire. The food was steaming hot, and warmed them inside.

"Better than pasties," said Gloria.

"Not as convenient, though," said Andy.

The faggots were highly spiced; they tasted good in the cold.

The fireworks didn't last very long, but the bonfire went on and on. By now the centre was glowing fiercely, and it cast out a great heat. Andy was torn between tending the fire, for it was burning in a circle and the edges needed throwing back into the centre, and staying with Gloria. He stayed, resisting the pull of the black figures who seemed to dance as they worked round the flames.

They sat looking into the fire. "It's like the other night," said Andy. He thought of the next time, and then after that . . . He was content for the moment.

She looked coy, not admitting any recollection of what had happened between them. They sat side by side, leaning towards each other, until the flames began to die down and the bonfire was just a heap of glowing embers.

Andy was working hard, preparing for the scholarship exam at the end of the term. He was seeing nothing of Duncan, as they had agreed, and so he was surprised to come home from the train after Saturday morning school and find him sitting down with his parents, drinking tea. "Oh, hullo," he said.

"Are you working this afternoon?"

"I was going to."

Duncan turned to Mr and Mrs Trewin, inquiringly.

"He's got to have a bit of time off," said his mum.

"Would you like to earn a pound?" asked Duncan.

"Yes, please," said Andy.

Duncan explained what it was all about. There was a big rugby match that afternoon at the sports field; Andy had in fact heard about it, and a lot of the boys were going. So were Gloria and her dad; they went to rugby a lot.

The *Yorkshire Evening Post* was sending its star sports reporter, Bill Harris, to cover the game, and he needed a runner. Would Andy like the job?

"What would I have to do?" he asked. He imagined a runner would have to be fast – and how far would he be required to run?

"All you've got to do is take his story as he writes it and phone it through to the *Post*," said Duncan. "It's money for jam."

"Did you say Bill Harris?" asked Mr Trewin.

"Yes."

"Not Big Bill Harris who played for Yorkshire before the war?"

"That's right. When he retired from county cricket he became a sports reporter."

"Slow left-arm bowler, I remember him well," said Mr Trewin. "Well I never."

The kick-off was at two-thirty, so Andy had to bolt his dinner. His parents fussed around him to get him off in time. In the car Duncan gave him a press badge; he had one himself, and on the windscreen a red notice said PRESS backwards.

"You're called a runner because you have to get to the phone before the other reporters," said Duncan. "If there's only one call box you need to be speedy, but you won't have any problems because the *Post* has an arrangement with a private house. I'll show you the house as we go by. You ring this number – he passed him a slip of paper – and reverse the charges. Then you ask for 'Copy' and dictate the report to a typist."

They drove up to the rugby ground and showed their press badges. The iron gates were opened wide and they were waved inside. Duncan was very matter-of-fact about it, but it gave Andy a thrill. He had never felt important before.

They went along the back of the crowd to the stand, where Duncan introduced him to Bill Harris. He was well over six feet tall. He sat hunched over a tiny typewriter on his knees, and was already tapping out the titles. The game was about to begin.

Duncan couldn't stay. "I've got a wedding," he said, raising his eyes to heaven. He slipped away.

Andy was fascinated to see a real writer at work, a professional whose words would be printed and sold before the day was out. The great man sat with a cigarette hanging out of his lips, and went *tap-tap-tap*, not even very fast. He was looking down at his typewriter when one of the players took a drop kick at the goal. The crowd roared.

"What was that?" asked Bill Harris, startled.

"A drop kick," said Andy.

"Who scored it?"

"I don't know," admitted Andy. Another pressman called out the player's name. *Tap-tap-tap* went the fingers on the typewriter.

From then on, Andy watched the game closely, so that he could provide any information he was asked for. At half-time Bill Harris rattled off a few more lines, turned the sheet out of the machine with a clicking noise, and handed it to Andy.

Andy hurried out of the stand. He saw Gloria and her dad, and gave them a wave, but he couldn't stop. He broke into a run along the side of the ground. It wasn't necessary, but it made him feel good.

His heart was beating fast. What if nobody answered the door? What if he had lost the phone number? What if he couldn't get through?

On the doorstep he took a deep breath. A bald-headed man opened the door; he was expecting Andy, and showed him the telephone in the hall. He dialled the operator, and asked for the transferred charge call. A voice said, "*York-shire Evening Post*" and he asked for "Copy". He dictated the report without taking it in at all.

He was back in time for the second half. He enjoyed watching rugby, it was just being made to play it on Wednesday afternoons that he didn't like. There were patches when it was very dull, with lots of line-ups and the ball being kicked into touch, and then suddenly the ball would come out of a scrum and be passed in a series of movements out along the wing for a final dash down the touch-line by the wing three-quarter. Or a tackle would stop a player just when it seemed that the way was open for him to score.

Both were away teams, and Andy had no reason to support one or the other, but his feelings became engaged in the game, boredom changing to excitement at the thrill of a try or disappointment at its interception, his hopes rising and falling. It was like watching a play.

When it was all over, Big Bill Harris wrote a new beginning to his story – Andy thought this was a very professional touch – and gave him the two sheets of paper. Andy joined the crowd streaming out of the ground as the light began to fade.

He felt no nervousness this time. When he got through, he said, "Oh, Copy, I've got a new intro," as though he'd been doing it all his life. "*Doncaster's dream of an unbeaten season was shattered this afternoon, when Hull snatched victory from them in the closing moments of an exciting game.*"

He relished Big Bill Harris's prose style. The copy typist read it back to him. He could picture her from her voice: young, blonde, a bit cheeky. He began to feel he was establishing a relationship with her, and then he had to ring off.

He walked to the bus stop; Duncan was presumably still at the wedding, and there was no sign of Gloria and her dad. There was a long queue for the buses. It began to drizzle, and the lights of cars gleamed on the wet roads.

His mum and dad wanted to know how it had gone. "It was easy," he said. He had done nothing, really.

"What was Bill Harris like?"

"Big."

"Did he speak to you?"

"Of course."

His dad believed that everything was a matter of knowing the right people. He had never known the right people, but Andy knew Duncan who knew Bill Harris who fixed him up with a job on the *Yorkshire Evening Post*. It was a good start.

If Andy won a scholarship to Cambridge, it would only partly be due to his own efforts. What really mattered was that he had Carrington working for him, and Carrington knew the tutors and dons.

Later, Mr Trewin cycled into Barnsby in the rain to buy a copy of the paper. When he came back, he spread it out on the table and found the report. He read it aloud, and then fetched scissors to cut it out.

"The first money you've earned," he said. "You'll never forget that."

It wasn't even as though I wrote it, thought Andy.

Because of bonfire night, he hadn't gone to the pictures with Gloria, and they missed the following Friday as well. He didn't mind. A double seat in the back of the cinema now seemed rather tame, and there was nowhere else to go. It was too cold and wet to go to Houghton Hill, or sit about on park benches or in shelters. Reg was going out with a girl from Woolworth's: he still made use of the pews in St Wilfred's church.

Andy didn't want any of this. He was waiting for the next opportunity of being alone with Gloria, either in his house or hers. But Mr and Mrs Trewin were always at home, and although Mr Butterfield went out a lot – every evening, Gloria said – his wife remained behind. On the few occasions when they went out together, Bobby was left in the house. However, Andy took the chance to get on with his work, and knew that one day they would be alone again. And then . . . his imagination ran away with him.

On the Saturday after the rugby match, Gloria called late in the afternoon. She had an invitation for Andy and the sixth form to an end-of-term party at the girls' school. Miss Baraclough was still trying hard to bring them together. It was signed by Dorothy Best.

Mrs Trewin was setting the table. "Won't you stay and have some tea with us?" she asked.

"Oh, thanks," said Gloria.

They talked about what Andy could do to get Old Man Harding to invite the sixth form girls to Bywaters. A New Year's celebration?

"Over my dead body," mimicked Andy.

A tennis party in the spring? A cricket match in the summer, with the boys playing left-handed?

"Why should they play left-handed?" asked Gloria, quick to take offence.

"We'd wipe the floor with you otherwise."

"We'd beat you at tennis."

They sat down to tea. It wasn't anything special, just bread and butter and jam, and Mrs Trewin's heavycake; none of the splits and cream, trifle and fruit cake there would have been if Gloria had been specially invited. To make a bit more of it, his mother opened a tin of sweetened condensed milk. Andy spread the thick, sticky milk on a slice of bread.

"Is that another Cornish habit?" Gloria asked, rather amused by it.

"Oh no, it's just a favourite of Andrew's, ever since he was tiny," said Mrs Trewin. "There used to be an advertisement before the war. *What, bread and milk at a party? – Yes, if it's Nestlés.* It was one of the first things he could say." She imitated the infant Andy, exaggerating the question in the voice and the stress on certain words: "*What,* bread and milk at a *par*-tee? He always loved it."

Gloria laughed and laughed. Andy felt rather stupid, and the milk on his bread began to ooze over the sides of the slice. He licked it where it was forming a big pearly drop about to fall. Even though he was careful, he could feel the stickiness around his lips and on his fingers.

He wished his mum wouldn't say things like that. He would never eat Nestlé's milk again.

"Hey, what were you doing at the match last Saturday?" asked Gloria, as soon as she had recovered enough to speak.

"I was a runner." He explained what he had done.

"How did you get the job?"

"It was through Duncan Smith," said his father.

No sooner had he spoken the name, than there was a ring on the bell. Mr Trewin went to the door, and then they heard Duncan's voice in the hall, "I was just passing by, I can't come in . . . well, just *two* minutes, quite literally."

"We were talking about you," said Mr Trewin. "I'd only just mentioned your name."

"*And pat he comes, like the catastrophe of the old comedy,*" said Duncan, entering the room. He turned to Andy. "Context?"

"King Lear." It was one of the set books.

"Too easy," said Duncan. "I hope you were saying nothing unkind about me."

Mr Trewin took it seriously. "Oh no, of course not. I was saying that you fixed up the job for Andrew last week."

"That's why I called." He opened his dark overcoat, and reached for his wallet. He took out a one pound note, and placed it with a flourish on the sideboard. The gesture had echoes of saloon bar gambling or gangster bosses. "*Here's remuneration for thee* – and I bet you can't give me the context of that."

"No," said Andy. Duncan was staring hard at Gloria, waiting to be introduced.

"Oh, this is Gloria," said Andy.

"La Tosca," said Duncan, with a smile. Andy hadn't worked out what he meant by calling her la Tosca, but he felt it was probably offensive.

Gloria frowned.

"Have some tea, Duncan," said Mrs Trewin.

"Set another place for him, Mother," said Mr Trewin. "Andrew, move around the table and sit with Gloria."

"No, really, I can't stay, I've got to be in Leeds by seven o'clock, I'm late already . . . well, just one cup."

He sat down at the table and Mrs Trewin poured his tea. Andy hoped that he wouldn't notice the bread and Nestlés milk. He suddenly felt that it was very childish, and Duncan was always so psychological about everything. He would die if his mum told the story of how he used to repeat the slogan, *What, bread and milk at a par-tee?*

Duncan talked – mostly about the wedding he had reported – until his tea had gone cold, and Mrs Trewin wanted to pour him a fresh cup. But he really *had* to be going. He gulped down the cold tea, and leaped to his feet. He looked at Gloria. "*Lovely* to meet you," he said, in a way that had so much charm it was somehow insulting.

"He'll never get to Leeds by seven o'clock," said Mr Trewin after he had left. "I hope he goes carefully."

Pavel started the metronome ticking on the piano, for no apparent reason. They'd had a game of chess running for several days; they kept it set up in a music practising room, close to the study. It was less likely to be knocked over there. They added a few moves to the game, and then Andy looked at his watch. He wanted to see the Old Man before the end of break.

He went along and knocked on the study door.

"Come in."

"Good morning, sir," said Andy. "I've had this letter from the girls' school, inviting the sixth form to a Christmas party. I thought it would be all right to accept?"

The Old Man grunted, and held out his hand for the letter. As he read it, Andy looked round to see if Valerie was at her desk in the corner. She wasn't there; she must spend the break somewhere else. Harding passed the letter back. "It's out of school hours, you can do as you like."

"But what about the boarders?"

"They can't go."

"That seems unfair."

"I can't help it. I'm responsible for them, and I can't be responsible if they're at a party at the girls' school."

"You could come too, sir."

He gave a short laugh. "Sometimes, *Trew*in, I think that you like to tease me."

"No, sir," exclaimed Andy innocently.

"You'd like to see me dancing with Miss Baraclough, would you?" He seemed more human than usual. "I'd only spoil the fun for you."

"Perhaps one of the younger members of staff could go?"

The Old Man shook his head. Andy expected a reminder that they would be ambassadors for t' school, but he didn't say anything.

"Sir?" he enquired.

"Yes, *Trew*in." In his voice was the note of resignation he always had when he pronounced – or mispronounced – Andy's name.

"Don't you think we ought to invite the girls back here sometime? We've had two invitations from them now."

"What for?"

"I thought we might have a dance, early next term. We could decorate the old schoolhouse."

"How would they get here?"

"They could hire a bus."

"The weather might be bad. Perhaps later in the year we could do something. I'll discuss it with Mrs Harding."

No wonder schools never changed, thought Andy. If the sixth-formers pushed for anything different, all the head had to do was stall for a few months and they would leave. Then he could begin stalling again with the next lot, and nothing was ever done.

"What's it like on the train now?" the Old Man asked.

That at least was something that had been done. "Very good," said Andy.

"No more rough-houses?"

"None." No one seemed to think of it any more. The system really worked.

In fact the whole school seemed different. It was less tense, less ready to explode over the smallest incident. Andy didn't feel that any credit for this was due to him. He thought the main reason was the return of teachers who knew what they were doing, and pupils came out of lessons feeling less bored and frustrated. There was really not much need for prefects now – which he thought was as it should be.

"And Pugsley?"

"He's putting everything into his rugby."

"Good."

Andy thought the Old Man wanted to say something else. Perhaps he remembered how Andy had been reluctant to be head boy, and wanted to tell him that he was doing a good job. Or perhaps he wanted to wish him good luck with his scholarship next week.

"Just one more thing," he said. "Before you go up to Cambridge – get your hair cut, lad."

"Yes, sir," he said.

In one of the narrow corridors he met Valerie. They were on the same side; they both stepped to the opposite side to let the other pass, and then back again. It was like a dance movement.

"Where do you spend your break?" he asked.

"With the kitchen staff."

"Come to the prefects' study one day."

She laughed and shook her head.

The butcher's shop in the High Street was lit up, and as he cycled past on his way home he saw Gloria inside talking to her dad. He swung around in the road and waited, just beyond the splash of light on the pavement.

There were Christmas trees outside the greengrocer's next door.

He wanted to have one more date with her before he went to Cambridge for the exam. But she didn't look very pleased when she saw him waiting.

They rode along together. "Shall we go to the pictures on Friday?" he suggested.

"No."

"Why not?" They had missed a few weeks, and he had thought that she would be glad to go.

"I don't want to."

"But why?"

"It's in Italian."

"It's got subtitles. Duncan says it's very good, it was made as the Germans retreated, so it's very realistic. It makes British films look very stuffy."

"Then you'd better *go* with Duncan," she said.

He was taken by surprise. "I want to go with you."

"I'm not going with *you*," she said, scathingly.

"Why?"

"I don't want any more to do with you."

They went on in silence, her whole body expressing resentment. They were dazzled by the headlights of an approaching car, and then they were plunged into darkness again.

"What have I done?" he asked, still puzzled by her attitude.

"You know."

"I don't. What's the matter?"

"I've finished with you."

Andy couldn't understand. He tried to get her to explain, but she wouldn't say any more. They passed his house, and the oak tree at the end of the lane, and reached her gate. He followed her right into the empty garage.

"What are you following me for?" she asked angrily. "Why don't you leave me alone?"

"Why do you say you've finished with me?" They stood

in the cold under a light bulb hanging from a piece of flex, amongst the garden tools and deck chairs, bicycles and stepladders and the oily patches on the floor. "You must have a reason."

"I'm not going out with nancy boys," she said. "I'm not sharing you with that . . . Duncan." She could hardly bring herself to speak the name.

"It's not like that," said Andy. She was completely mistaken.

"You care more about him than you do about me."

"That's not true."

"I always knew you were like that."

"But I'm not," said Andy. "You know I'm not."

"It doesn't really surprise me, I always said you were effeminate." He tried to take hold of her and she fought him off. "I should never have gone out with you."

"You've got it all wrong," he said. "He's just a friend."

"What are you doing in his car, then, parked outside your house until all hours of the night? I've heard about it."

"We just talk."

"Yes, people are talking too."

"They ought to mind their own business."

"I've found out a lot about him. Did you know he's always hanging around the bar of the Houghton Arms? Did you know he used to hang around the youth club until the police warned him off? I reckon I know more about him than you do. Why's he always rushing off to Leeds, I'd like to know?"

He was still trying to hold her arms, and she was still pushing him away. "You don't understand," he said.

"I understand more than you do. He came worming his way into your family, making your mum and dad think what a nice friend he was for you. And you – you're just dazzled by him. When he came in last Saturday, you behaved quite different. It made me sick."

He's a friend, thought Andy. That was all, there was nothing more to it.

"He can't stand *me*, of course," she went on. "Because he knows I can see through him."

"There's no need to be jealous."

"Jealous," she scoffed. "I'm not jealous of *him*."

She finally broke away and rushed out of the garage towards the side door of the house. She turned on the step. "He *disgusts* me," she called out. "And so do you."

Andy stood still for a moment. Then he scuffed the oil off the bottom of his shoes, got on his bike and rode away. He felt shattered.

Mrs Saxon answered the door. Her face looked hard and grey, quite unlike the woman he'd met earlier in the term. When he had seen her before, Duncan had been there, calling her an angel and asking her for tea and scones, and her face had lit up.

It didn't light up when she saw Andy on the doorstep. "Mr Smith isn't at home," she said. "No, I don't know when he'll be back." She closed the door.

He went again on his way from the station after Saturday school. There was the same reponse. "I don't know where he is," she said coldly. "He's probably gone for the weekend."

Later in the afternoon he went back into town with his parents on the bus. They went to Pogsons the Outfitters to buy him a suit. They looked at a black jacket and striped trousers. "You'd look like an undertaker in that, boy," said his dad. There wasn't much choice, just navy-blue and grey. He picked a medium grey, and tried it on.

He looked at himself in the full-length mirror. The suit was slightly too big for him, the trousers very wide. It looked as though he'd just been demobbed from the army, and issued with a civilian suit from stock, except that he looked too young.

Then his mum wanted to buy him a dressing-gown. "I won't need it," he said.

"You will in college," she said. "You might have to cross the quadrangle to go to the toilet."

"I'll put on my raincoat."

"I'm sure everyone else will have one."

They bought him a plum-red dressing-gown with navy-blue collar and cuffs. The two purchases seemed very expensive, and used up all their clothing coupons.

It was almost dark when they got off the bus, but Andy thought there was a car parked outside their house. As they got nearer he could see that it was the Standard Ten. Duncan got out. "I won't delay you, I really must dash," he said. "But I couldn't let Andrew go off to Cambridge without wishing him good luck."

"Come on in," said Andy's dad.

"I literally can't stay more than *two* minutes."

"I'm just putting the kettle on," said his mum.

They were standing in the hall beneath the light, Andy with the two floppy, brown-paper parcels in his arms.

"What have we here?" asked Duncan.

"Just some clothes."

"It's his new suit for Cambridge," said his mum. "Go and try it on, dear, and show it to Duncan."

"He doesn't want to see it," said Andy. He felt too much fuss was being made over the suit; he bet nobody else bought a suit specially for an exam.

"But I'd *love* to," said Duncan, as though it was the greatest treat.

Andy went up to his bedroom to change, and when he came down they were all in the living room. He tried to walk in casually, his hands in his pockets. He felt clownish.

"Oh *yes*," said Duncan, appreciatively.

"Do you think it's right?" asked Mr Trewin.

"*Very* Cambridge."

Andy knew he was making fun of him, but his dad was reassured. "That's all right then," he said. "I didn't want him looking like a tailor's dummy."

Duncan went on to examine him rather more critically. "I think perhaps it needs some colour to brighten it up, just a *suspicion* of red at the neck."

"I thought I'd wear my school tie."

Duncan jumped up. "Look, I've got the world's largest collection of ties. Let's go and pick out a few."

"But you're in a hurry."

"That can wait." And with apologies to Mr and Mrs Trewin and promises to be back within *five* minutes, they hurried out to the car.

Duncan unlocked the door of the house in Church Walk, and they went up the stairs. His bedroom was down the landing from the sitting room at the front. He switched on the light. It was quite chaotic, and draped over the mirror of the dressing table were dozens of brightly-coloured ties. He opened the wardrobe, and took out several hangers, each crammed with more ties, hanging like streamers from the rail. Andy had never seen so many ties before; he could easily believe that it *was* the world's largest collection.

"All my friends laugh at my ties," said Duncan. "I really don't know why." He started to flick through them, occasionally pulling out one he thought suitable.

"Duncan."

"Mmm?" he said, concentrating on his choice.

"People are talking about you."

He licked a finger, and brushed it along his eyebrow. "Naturally," he said. "My public, bless them."

"Seriously," said Andy.

"What are they saying?" he asked. He kept adding ties to the pile of possible ones on the bed. There were stripes and patterns, woven ones and tartans.

"They say the police have warned you to keep away from the youth club."

"Lies," said Duncan. "I sometimes help at the church youth club, but I haven't been recently, I've been too busy. No one has warned me off."

"That's what they're saying."

"Typical small-town gossip. My God, I can't wait to get to London."

"Why do you go to Leeds so often?"

"Because I have friends there. Are they talking about that too?"

"Yes."

"I'm staying with them until tomorrow evening."

"I see."

"I'm sorry to disappoint you, but it's nothing very dramatic. We shall have a meal and then go out to someone else's flat. There may be a party, but nothing like the orgies you imagine."

"I don't," said Andy.

He picked out a tie. "Oh, I like that," he said, holding it against Andy's suit. "Let's try it on."

It was a Paisley design, purple and red in colour. Andy took off his old tie, and Duncan passed the new one around his neck and under the collar. He tied the knot, frowning with concentration, and slid it up to the neck. He smoothed down the collar.

"Do you have a particular friend in Leeds?" Andy asked.

"No one special."

He took a clean white handkerchief, and pressed it into Andy's breast pocket. He adjusted the knot of the tie, and let his hands rest on his shoulders. He looked into his eyes, and gave him a wink. "Good luck," he said.

Andy arrived in Cambridge late in the afternoon, when all the lights were beginning to shine thickly through the gloom. He took a taxi to his college, and looked out at the buildings shrouded in fog, the busy streets. The taxi stopped in a lane, with high walls on either side.

He got out and paid the driver.

He was standing in front of a gatehouse; he could just make out the tower above the surrounding roofs. There was an iron lamp over the arch, and it cast a yellowish light on to the steps and doorway. The great metal-studded wooden doors were closed, but there was a small door cut into them; this was open.

He stepped through and went into the porters' lodge. He

147

was given some information sheets, a key and instructions how to find his rooms.

The porter, who looked rather like Andy's dad, called him *sir*. It was quite a shock; he even glanced around to see if the man was addressing someone else. He didn't like calling teachers *sir*, and after the first surprise he didn't want anyone to call him *sir*. The porter came out of his warm lodge to show him the way.

He was in a courtyard; a path led across it to a dimly-lit arched opening. There were tall windows with stained glass, just showing through the mist. There was another arched opening to the right, and the porter directed him to this.

He passed through into a second court, and found the staircase. At the entrance the names of the occupants were painted in white lettering on black. His rooms were on the ground floor, and were normally occupied by R. H. S. Gorton. He wondered who he was. He unlocked the outer door, opened the inner door, and switched on the light.

It was a long, low room, with a mullioned window and leaded lights. There was an open fireplace; the grate was empty and the room was very cold. The furniture looked well-used but comfortable; there were plenty of book-shelves, and several table lamps. He went and looked in the small bedroom leading from it, and dropped his case on a chair.

He sat down in one of the armchairs to get the feel of the room. He could imagine the characters in a Forster novel, Rickie and Ansell, in just such a room, discussing whether objects exist only when there is someone to look at them, or whether they have a real existence of their own. '*The cow is there,' said Ansell, lighting a match and holding it out over the carpet.* Was the cow there or not? And what about R. H. S. Gorton? Did he exist apart from his rooms during the vacation? Did Andy exist for him?

He hoped he would have a question on Forster in the exam. He got up and tried to establish more about the usual inhabitant of the room. From his books, he seemed to be a scientist with an interest in music. It looked as though he had walked out a few minutes earlier; there was half a bottle of sherry on top of a cupboard, and several invitations still propped on the mantelshelf. He played squash; there was a racket in the corner.

Yes, thought Andy, he could live very happily in a room like this. Then he shivered; it was bitterly cold. There was a bucket of coal and a gas poker, and he lit a fire. It only needed buttered buns to complete the scene.

He had nearly two hours before hall, which he assumed was dinner. He read for a while, and then stared into the fire, which by now was glowing warmly. It made him think of Gloria. He couldn't believe she meant what she had said. She'd get over it, and come back to him.

Later, he explored the staircase, and found a communal kitchen, a bathroom and toilet. Then he explored the college, finding the hall, which at first glance he mistook for the chapel. He walked through empty courts and ended up on a bridge over the river; the mist lay across the water and the backs, and the trees were dripping moisture.

A bell clanged, and he joined the people going to dinner. There was quite a crowd, appearing from different courts and staircases. The hall was now lit up, and he found a place at one of the long tables. There were a few dons at the high table, and some undergraduates still in college – he could pick them out because they wore gowns. He supposed everyone else was like himself, up for the scholarship.

A college servant struck a gong, and all the chatter and noise died away, except for the scraping of benches as people stood up. There was a long grace in Latin – Carrington had recited the whole of it to him one day – and then more scraping as everyone sat down. The conversation began again, and waiters came around with bowls of soup.

He glanced up at the roof. It had open beams painted red, with gilt stars between them, and carved wooden angels.

The top half of the walls were painted in a pattern of red and green; it looked like Christmas wrapping paper. There were gothic windows, with coats-of-arms in stained glass, and a great fireplace. There was also, in a different style, lots of panelling and gilt-framed portraits. It was strange, eating in a place like this.

He exchanged a few remarks with the boy next to him, about where they were from and what subjects they were doing. Most people were in groups from the same school, where they already knew each other. Some of them seemed very much at home, calling for the waiter who served drinks and ordering half-pints of beer. It came in pewter mugs.

The meat dish was followed by a savoury, sardines on toast. Andy was disappointed; he liked his pudding. He watched the serving hatch beneath the gallery, but no puddings appeared. He went along to the junior common room, where people seemed to group themselves according to subject. This gave him a chance to size up the competition.

The boys were mostly from public schools. They were loud and confident, and alarmingly well-read. It was easy enough to shine in a small country grammar school, thought Andy. But he couldn't really expect to compete with these sophisticates. There was one boy from Eton – he wore a club tie and fawn waistcoat – and because he was from Eton everyone else seemed to respect him.

Andy lost all his confidence. He didn't know why he had applied to Cambridge; it was only because Carrington was pushing him. It was such a masculine place, he hadn't seen a woman since he had arrived. It was just like Bywaters, only on a grander scale. He'd much rather go to a university like Leeds, where there were girls as well as men.

He woke up in the morning to hear somebody moving around in the outer room. It took him a moment to realise where he was; in the morning light he could see thick bars outside the window, which opened into the lane. He put on his plum and navy dressing-gown – his mum had been quite right – and went out.

A college bedmaker was on her knees in front of the fireplace, cleaning out the grate. Carrington had told him that bedmakers were chosen for their age and ugliness, and this lady was no exception to the rule. But he was glad to see her, and wished her good morning and asked whether it was always foggy in Cambridge. She said it was. He asked if she was married and whether she had any family, and she answered briefly, as though he was being cheeky.

He dressed and went to the hall for breakfast. There followed a day of writing answer papers and attending interviews. He talked about Elizabethan dramatists and romantic poets, and in what he said he heard Carrington's voice, and more often Duncan's voice, and occasionally his own.

He didn't mind being tested. It was a game, and if you knew the rules of the game and played it fairly well, you could enjoy it. And there was a question on the modern novel which gave him his chance to write about Forster.

Old Man Harding always let the sixth formers have time off in the week before Christmas to work at the Post Office. Andy met Reg outside the Post Office building just before eight. A few of the boys going to catch the train were in the street, and it felt good to see them going to school while he was going to work. He hoped to earn between two and three pounds during the Christmas rush. They went into the sorting room and signed on.

It was a large bare room, with rows of pigeon-holes and metal frames hung with mail bags. One man was throwing packets into them, very expertly. There were great heaps on the floor.

Andy and Reg were assigned to a postman called Harry, dealing with parcel deliveries. He was sorting the parcels into local districts, and they carried them out to a builder's lorry, which had been hired with its driver for the busy period. They filled up the back of the lorry, piling them high and covering them with a tarpaulin.

Then off they went around the suburbs of the town. It was very cold, with a biting wind and some sleety rain. Reg, who had been on the post before, complained about the lorry; last year they had had a furniture van, which gave them more shelter. Harry stayed on the back, getting the parcels into order and handing them down to Andy and Reg to deliver. Every so often he would beat his arms around his body.

Their breath steamed in the cold air. They went up garden paths and knocked on doors, but they didn't walk far enough to warm up. Andy's fingers were numb inside his khaki gloves.

About the middle of the morning he called at his own house, with a parcel from Aunt Mary; it would be the Trewins' first Christmas in Yorkshire, as his dad had used up all his leave. "Any post?" he asked his mum. He was waiting to hear from Cambridge.

"Only a Christmas card." She passed him an envelope and he shoved it in his pocket. She wanted them to come in for a drink, but Harry wouldn't stop. He stood up in the back of the lorry and cracked an imaginary whip, as though he were driving a sleigh.

Andy climbed over the tailboard and they were off to the next part of the town, the wind blowing keen against their faces. He sat down amongst the parcels and took the envelope out of his pocket. It was a card from Duncan, posted in London. Opposite the printed greeting he had scrawled: *I've an interview with the News Chronicle, and there are one or two other possibilities. I shall stay on in London until after Christmas, but whatever happens I'll be back in Barnsby for the New Year. Love, Duncan.*

The lorry stopped. They climbed down and began delivering. The number of parcels on the back never seemed to decrease, but gradually there was more space on board, and the pile diminished until there were only a few left in the corner, the ones they hadn't been able to find or had overlooked – these could go the rounds again tomorrow. They got back into the depot at a quarter past two.

They spent an hour's break at Reg's, and in the afternoon took out the handcart. It was painted black and post-office red; it had a big wicker lid and wheels like a pony trap. It wasn't as cold as on the back of the lorry. There was a Christmas atmosphere, as it began to get dark in the middle of the afternoon and the lights went on.

It was fun delivering parcels around the town, pushing the cart and seeing all the people in the streets, going into shops and wishing the salesgirls a merry Christmas.

There was a hard frost during the night, and when he rode into work the next morning the puddles were thick with ice; the grass in the verges was stiff and white. The pavements were slippery, and some of the gates stuck, frozen to the posts. It slowed them down, and there were more parcels than ever. It was a quarter to three before they finished the lorry round, and nearly six o'clock before they left the post office for the day.

When he got home, his mum and dad were waiting for him; they seemed apprehensive. "There's a letter for you from Cambridge," his dad said. "We haven't opened it."

He broke open the envelope, and took in the contents at a glance. The college was offering him a scholarship. He showed it to his parents.

"Well done, boy," said his dad, with quiet satisfaction. "You've shown them."

His mum was more excited. She said it was the best Christmas present they could have had. Andy read the letter through word for word. His first thought was that he wanted to tell Duncan, but he was in London. He ought to tell Carrington, though he felt sure that he would have heard already through his contacts with the college.

And then he felt as his dad had, satisfaction that he had done it. *He had shown them*. He thought of all those others in the junior common room, up for an English scholarship. And the college had chosen *him*.

He had no time to dwell on it. He had to rush to change into his new suit and cycle back into town for the end-of-term party at the girls' school.

The last time he had been in the grammar school hall was when he had met Duncan. It looked quite different now. There was a large Christmas tree by the side of the stage, covered with tinsel, baubles and candles; the gallery was decorated with paper-chains and balloons. There was a lot of holly everywhere – the school grounds were full of bushes – but he couldn't see any mistletoe.

The boys who had already arrived were standing together, and the girls formed separate groups; there were far more girls than boys. He saw Gloria at once, he couldn't miss her. Her shoulders were bare. There was absolutely nothing on them, not even a neckband or a strap. He couldn't see how the dress stayed up. It went over her bust and under her arms, hugging her tight to the waist, and then it flared away in a full-length skirt. She must have been shopping in Leeds again.

She tried to pretend that she hadn't seen him, but he went across to her. He still couldn't believe that she meant what she had said. He could tell her about his scholarship.

"Gloria," he said, standing almost in front of her, giving her the chance to be friends.

She frowned and with a toss of her head turned her back on him. Her long skirt swirled around.

"Aren't you talking to me?"

She didn't answer, but walked down the hall to join another girl. He watched her bare shoulders go.

It was a moment or two before he realised that Dorothy was standing by him. As head girl, she welcomed him and the other boys. She was wearing a sober plaid dress which buttoned up to the neck. She had an air about her; she was very much head girl.

It was nearly six months since he had gone out with her: she looked at least a year older. They hadn't spoken since that day, and they made no reference to it now. He wondered if she was thinking about it; if she was, she didn't give any sign. He felt a bit embarrassed about it, and also rather pleased to think that he had burrowed beneath that woollen plaid dress. He suddenly thought that really she was very attractive. He wouldn't mind going out with her again.

They talked about universities; she had applied to several but had not yet had any replies. She seemed confident that she would be accepted. She would try for a county major award in the summer. He didn't say anything about his scholarship, keeping it for later. But he knew that she would appreciate it; she understood what it meant.

Her voice was still very flat Yorkshire; he thought it made her interesting. He felt that he too was more than six months older. He would be able to talk to her now. He had even read *To the Lighthouse*, and had several ideas about it.

But before he could tell her, she had suggested that they ought to be getting the two schools to mix, and they started making introductions. Then Miss Baraclough took charge, and with Miss Mottram the games mistress operating the gramophone, she invited them all to dance the Tom Jones. Andy took Dorothy as his partner, but it was a dance in which everyone eventually partners everyone else, the idea being to throw people together. The boys didn't know the dance very well and stumbled through it, the girls pulling and pushing them to face the right partner, and they all laughed and began to get to know one another.

Andy could see Gloria coming down the line; she would soon be his partner. When he turned round to face her and take her hand, she looked at him without seeing him, a haughty expression on her face. He ended up with Dorothy again.

Miss Baraclough kept to a strict programme of games and dances. Reg reported that all the doors out of the hall were locked; there was no sneaking off into a classroom, for a quick drag or a snog. The only way out was by the front entrance, and there were two teachers there, one on either side of the door.

Some of the games were more suitable for a children's party. They played them rather mockingly; Sowerby and Clark began muttering about *Hyde Park*, and Reg asked loudly, "Yes, what about *Hyde Park*?" and one or two of the girls joined in and repeated it. Andy had played it last January at a party in the St John Ambulance hall. Each boy sat on a chair with a girl on his lap, and all the lights went out. One boy was a policeman with a torch. If he shone it on any couple and they were necking, he changed places with the boy. It was a good game.

But Miss Baraclough refused to hear; they finished *The Parson's Cat*, and the winning girl was awarded a neatly wrapped bar of chocolate from the Christmas tree. They went straight into a military two-step.

After that, a door was unlocked, and they walked through part of the school to the domestic science room. Andy walked up the stairs with Dorothy beside him. He thought how cool and elegant she was as she mounted the steps; he felt very attracted towards her. They had been together most of the evening. He couldn't believe that he had once been out with her.

The food made up for the games; none of the boys had seen a display like it. The girls must have saved up from their rations since the beginning of term. Andy followed Dorothy's example, took a plate and helped himself. They moved to one side of the room; she still wished to be with him.

"How are you going home?" he asked, thinking that she would be on her bicycle and he could ride back with her. He didn't want anyone else to ask her first.

"I'm being met," she said.

"By your dad?"

"No."

"Who by?"

"My boyfriend," she said. And she went on to explain, in her flat Yorkshire voice, that her older brother was at Leeds University and he had brought a friend home during the last long vacation. His name was Graham, he was reading English, and she had become friendly with him. He was staying over Christmas. He couldn't come to the party because only the sixth form had been invited.

Andy hated him.

He knew that he couldn't expect Dorothy to wait patiently for him until he lost interest in Gloria – or Gloria lost interest in him – and then pick up again just where they had left off. But the food in his mouth lost all its taste. He could hardly swallow.

He tried to control his feelings, to carry on talking quite normally, as though nothing had happened. Dorothy said she ought to circulate.

The boys demolished every bit of food – the boarders would have enjoyed it – and then they returned to the hall for more games and dancing. Andy was tired after two days on the parcels lorry, and the excitement of the scholarship news had quickly worn off. He had lost Gloria, and he had lost Dorothy; the party was a failure.

It became a little more lively towards the end. They all danced a samba, holding on to the waist of the person in front, and the girl who was leading it took them around the hall, snaking along the corridor and up the stairs, through the cookery room and back to the hall. Then they joined hands and sang Auld Lang Syne, and threw balloons and paper-chains into the air.

Andy and Reg had grabbed two girls in the samba. They were in the lower sixth, and were called Cathy and Viv. "Can we take you home?" asked Reg, as they threw off the paper-chains that had dropped over them. The two girls looked at each other, and burst out laughing.

As they waited for the girls, Andy watched the others leave. Dorothy hurried away with a wave; Gloria ignored him as she walked past with Peter Pugsley, her overcoat covering her bare shoulders. It hurt to see them go off together. Cathy and Viv came back from the cloakroom. They laughed again as they saw the boys.

Outside the school they switched over, and Andy walked along with Viv. He put his arm around her waist. The temperature hadn't risen much above freezing all day, and now the frost was biting hard again. The lights of the town sparkled clear. He could feel her warmth.

They both lived near the centre of the town. Reg stopped in Church Walk, and Andy glanced up at the dark windows of the first floor at number five. "Have you ever been inside the church at night?" Reg asked. "It's very spooky."

The girls just giggled.

"Shall we go in?"

"It's locked."

"I've got a key," and he produced it from his pocket.

They went up the path between the tombstones; there was enough light from the frosty sky to see by. The girls giggled again, but more nervously, as they entered the porch. Reg put the key in the lock, and turned. The door creaked as he pushed it open.

The girls squealed, and pulled back, holding on to each other. "It's all right," said Reg. "Come on."

Andy held Viv by the hand, and walked into the pitch darkness of the church. He held the other hand up in front of him in case he bumped in to anything.

"Where are you?" he whispered.

"Here," hissed Reg.

The girls were making tiny noises; it was difficult to tell whether it was suppressed laughter, or whether they were really scared.

They felt their way to the back pew, and all four of them sat in a row. There was a sudden scampering noise. "Oh," Viv gasped, sucking in her breath and holding it. She froze. Andy could feel the hair standing up on the back of his neck, yet he knew it was only a mouse or a bird on the roof. He held her protectively; he could feel her heart beating fast.

She began to breathe normally again. He heard Reg murmuring something, and Cathy giggled. Viv pulled away to know what it was about. He drew her back.

"Oh," she gasped again.

"What's the matter?"

"Your hand's cold."

She said it aloud, and it started Cathy off into another bout of laughing. They settled down after a while, and the church was still and quiet.

Then Cathy began to make demurring noises. "I don't like it here, it's too cold," she suddenly announced. "I want to go."

Reg was appealing to her to stay, but she pulled away and a dark shape loomed over Andy. She was trying to pull Viv away too. "Come on," she said. "My dad'll play murder."

Viv drew away, and they brushed past his knees in the pew. The girls felt their way out of the church, stumbling against the table with the magazines and breaking into another fit of giggles. There was a rush of cold air as the door opened, and then it slammed behind them.

Andy and Reg were alone in the church. "Brown Cows," said Reg, "they're all the same. What happened to Gloria this evening?"

"I've finished with her," said Andy. Then he added more truthfully, "Well, she finished with me."

"I don't know why you bother with them."

If only, thought Andy. If only he could find the right person, all he felt about Gloria and all he felt about Duncan, rolled together in one. He wondered if it would ever be possible.

"Shopgirls are best," said Reg.

Perhaps he had already missed his chance; perhaps Dorothy could have been the one, if he hadn't made such a mess of it.